MY SINFUL TEMPTATION

A NOVELLA IN THE SINFUL MEN SERIES

LAUREN BLAKELY

Copyright © 2020 by Lauren Blakely

Cover Art by Shana Yasmin and Design by Kate Farlow

All rights reserved. No part of this book may be reproduced or transmitted in any form or by any means whatsoever without express written permission from the author, except in the case of brief quotations embodied in critical articles and reviews. Names, characters, places, brands, media, and incidents are either the product of the author's imagination or are used fictitiously. The author acknowledges the trademarked status and trademark owners of various products referenced in this work of fiction, which have been used without permission. The publication/use of these trademarks is not authorized, associated with, or sponsored by the trademark owners. This is a work of fiction. Names, characters, business, events and incidents are the products of the author's imagination. Any resemblance to actual persons, living or dead, or actual events is purely coincidental. Without in any way limiting the author's exclusive rights under copyright, any use of this publication to "train" generative artificial intelligence (AI) technologies to generate text is expressly prohibited. The author reserves all rights to license uses of this work for generative AI training and development of machine learning language models.

ABOUT

A brand new story in the sexy, emotional Sinful Men series! Devour this sensual friends-to-lovers romance from #1 New York Times Bestselling author Lauren Blakely...

Just because you want a woman doesn't mean you get to have her.

I've been lusting after Mindy Gamble since the night I met her, but romance was never in the cards. Working to crack a case was the only order of the day.

Now, a year later, she's one of my closest friends. The feisty, no-nonsense, sexy-as-hell blonde that I just want to slap my handcuffs on and do bad things to.

I resist though, since I need her too much as a friend. Until the night all my resistance cracks, and we fall into bed together.

And I start thinking we can maybe find a way to make this work. Until she tells me she's leaving town...

MY SINFUL TEMPTATION
A NOVELLA IN THE SINFUL MEN SERIES

By Lauren Blakely

To be the first to find out when all of my upcoming books go live click here!

PRO TIP: Add lauren@laurenblakely.com to your contacts before signing up to make sure the emails go to your inbox!

Did you know this book is also available in audio and paperback on all major retailers? Go to my website for links!

This is an emotional, suspenseful series, with high-stakes action and consequences. For content warnings go to my web site.

1

MINDY

I had a good feeling about today. Maybe it would be a tough one, but ultimately things would be all right.

Between my stint in the Army and my years working in private security, I'd learned to trust my instincts. They were attuned to trouble, and it was a welcome change to zero in on something different. Something good, even.

That was why I ignored the accessorized outfit I'd picked out last night and hung on the hook on the closet door, as I usually did.

Instead, I reached for something less somber, a combo more suited to the Nevada day than an air-conditioned casino.

Blue instead of black. Well, that *was* a little less somber. Swishing the skirt to shake out the back-of-the-closet wrinkles, I slid it on and gave myself a cursory glance in the mirror, then a thumbs-up. I smoothed my hair and checked for lipstick on my teeth. I grabbed the extra pack of tissues from the dresser and put them in my bag.

Because while I was optimistic about the day, I didn't kid myself that there wouldn't be tears—if not from me, then from someone I cared about.

The Sloan siblings had become dear to me, and not only because my best friend, Brent, had married into the family. They'd traveled to hell and back, enduring tragedy and upheaval that would tear any family apart, but they'd come out of it closer than ever.

As I headed to the door, I glanced at the pictures of my sisters in Colorado that lined the hall. I missed them terribly, but not quite as much as I detested snow. In my favorite picture of us, we had our arms around each other and a fresh dusting of powder on our jackets and in our hair, and the camera had caught me glaring at the wretched white stuff like it had personally offended me—which it had, by simply existing.

My sisters teased me mercilessly about that picture, and I grinned like I always did when I thought about it.

I'd call Audrey tonight, catch up with her, and maybe talk to Celia, hands down the world's most adorable five-year-old. No kid was cuter, and I never hung up the phone without a smile at some clever or endearing thing she'd told me.

As I left, the hot and dry Las Vegas air evaporated all my thoughts about snow when I grabbed my car from the parking garage and drove toward the edge of town, stopping at a roped-off empty piece of land. The only thing left of the White Box Gentleman's Club was the pitted parking lot full of vehicles, everything from town cars to news vans. The property where the bar had stood was now a bare patch of plowed ground.

I snagged a spot at the end of the row. Groups of people were clustered on the empty lot, and I headed that way. I hadn't gone far when a Nissan LEAF hummed past me and zipped into the empty space beside my car. I recognized the compact hatchback—by sight, and by the sound of its battery-powered engine—and I bit back a smile as Detective John Winston climbed out. He'd heard every joke I could make about his vehicle—about finding a place to plug in his car while on a stakeout, about the electric motor being good for sneaking up on criminals.

I waited for him to catch up to me so we could walk over together to join the crowd, and as he reached me, I made a big show of checking my watch. "Right on the dot, as usual. You plan that, don't you—arriving not a minute too soon or a moment too late?"

He kept a straight face, but his blue eyes twinkled. "What if I do? And note that we are walking over together, Miss Punctuality."

With a shrug, I fell into step with him. "Too much 'hurry up and wait' during my formative years. So it goes when your dad is a colonel. You know, 'If you're not ten minutes early, you're late,' and all that."

"Nothing wrong with punctuality. It's an admirable trait."

"It is." I nodded with the same overly serious demeanor. Then I shrugged it off. "Now I guess it's my little rebellion—seeing how close I can arrive without being late."

"Whoa." He made a *down, girl* motion, but he was smiling. "I know this is Las Vegas, but don't go too wild now."

I leaned over and confessed in a whisper, "Sometimes when I'm early, I sit in my car in the parking lot listening to a few minutes of a podcast instead of going in and twiddling my thumbs until the meeting or whatever starts."

"I know what you need." His voice dropped low, and he leaned closer too, like he was offering me drugs. "I have an app that tells me my ETA to the minute. You could speed up or slow down accordingly. Want me to send you a download link?"

I didn't know how the man did it, but he made trading apps sound . . . like an invitation to something more.

To something like going wild with Detective John Winston.

Where had that come from? I hadn't had a thought like that in a long while. There had been a time when I'd thought maybe there was a little spark between us, when I'd hoped it might catch fire...

But that had not been in the cards. Friendship was our winning hand, it turned out. So I embraced that, even as his gravelly voice and his deep blue eyes made my skin tingle.

"Sure. Send it to me," I said, since it was better to banter than to dwell on how damn good he smelled, clean and woodsy and thoroughly masculine. Because that also delivered the tingles. "Do you also have one that detects when and how to avoid small talk with colleagues?"

He groaned. "Small talk is the bane of my existence. Why do you think I have that app? When I slow down my drive, it's so I won't have time to make small talk."

I scoffed. "I call bullshit. Cops must have the get-there-ASAP reflex etched into them as rookies."

It was his turn to shrug. "I'm a detective now. By the time I get a call, a minute or two won't make a difference."

He caught himself with a guilty grimace and glanced toward the crowd gathered around the staked-off square of dirt. "Sorry. I'm going to lose my sensitivity merit badge one of these days."

I swerved enough to bump his shoulder with

mine. "You don't have to apologize to me for dark humor. Or a dark side, such as it is." We were still out of earshot. The Sloans were gathered on the far side of the lot, along with the mayor and a few other notables. "But . . . time and place."

"There's a time and place for everything," he said, his eyes locking with mine for a sliver of a second.

I stepped onto the stone path. The heel of my shoe caught in the gravel, and I stumbled. Lashing out, I grabbed the only thing in reach—John's arm.

Whoa.

I'd seen those muscles in the gym. Why was touching them different? How could the way he felt, even through his sport coat sleeve—or especially through his sleeve, touching what no one else could see—affect me on a deeper level than ogling him in the gym, admiring the curves of his arms, the washboard abs, the hard planes of his muscled back, ever had?

Ah, crap. I did not need to be thinking this today.

Today, I was here to support my friends. Not to cop a feel of my friendly neighborhood detective.

"Careful there. It gets uneven where the building was bulldozed," he said.

"Good riddance to bad rubbish," I said under my breath. The White Box had been an unsavory establishment. A gentlemen's club that had never seen a gentleman. And that was before factoring in the mob boss who'd run the place.

"No argument from me. Or anyone on the police force, really."

We jostled through the crowd until we were close to the front where we could see the Sloans gathered to the side of a podium with a microphone. A patch of bare earth had been roped off and a pristine shovel set aside for the formality of turning the first shovelful of dirt—and the photo op that would follow.

I waved to Brent. His wife, Shannon, stood closer to her brothers, but Brent was an arm's length away if she needed his support. I could imagine him being that way with their son too, who'd just started to walk—giving both independence and a safety net at the same time.

Next to them was John's sister, Sophie. She'd married into the family—she was Sophie Sloan now, married to Shannon's brother Ryan. Spotting John, she turned on a beaming smile and . . .

"Damn. I think she gets bigger every time I see her," John said, keeping his voice down.

Even with the low volume, I teased him. "You know that sensitivity merit badge you were worried about?" I held out my hand, palm up, and wiggled my fingers in a demand. "Hand it over, Winston."

Though, I had to admit, when she stood in profile like that, Sophie's belly was awe-inspiring.

My gaze drifted across the line of siblings and their significant others. These were my friends—finding love, creating homes together, and having babies.

Enabling my favorite hobby—aunting.

I was a most excellent aunt.

John exchanged waves with his sister, then undid the button at his collar, his only concession to the heat. Undone buttons looked damn good on him.

"Did you want to go up there with Sophie?" I asked, distracted by his off-center tie.

He looked at me, his eyes alight with surprise. "No. She's with Ryan and the family."

I wondered if he felt any of the same things I did, only more so, because Sophie was his little sister. The feeling of being on the outskirts of someplace busy and bustling, on the fringes of something special in this group of family and friends brought together by a connection that, once tragic, had finally come full circle.

"Are you ready to be Uncle John?" I asked, segueing back to Sophie's unignorable belly.

He gave a snort. "'Uncle John' sounds like an old codger with cardigans and weird nose hair who swears he can forecast the weather with his bum knee."

"I didn't know you could predict the weather," I said cheekily.

He scoffed. "That's the part you home in on? The weather bit? You wound me, Gamble. Wound me."

Laughing, I bumped him with my shoulder. "Can't wait to see those cardigans. Wear one to the gym next time, will you?"

"Don't tempt me. I just might now."

I grinned. Someone tapped the microphone up front, and a hush fell over the crowd. A woman I didn't know—maybe a PR person—introduced the mayor, who welcomed everyone and then introduced Michael, who would say a few words on behalf of the family.

Michael shook the mayor's hand, his expression serious. He took his responsibility as the oldest Sloan sibling very seriously, and today was no different. He stepped up to the mic and began to speak, solemn but not grim. He seemed almost peaceful. As I looked at Shannon, Colin, and Ryan, that feeling seemed to be shared among them.

"Thank you all for coming. More than fifteen months ago, there was a building here. One with uncomfortable, even painful associations for many—not just me and my family. The people who ran that place left a trail of wreckage behind them, hurting far too many innocent families. They can't hurt anyone now, and though the White Box club had been shut down for a while, it seemed nobody wanted it. But we did. My brothers and my sister and I bought that boarded-up property. We had no dreams of opening a restaurant or club. We thought it was time that building came down, and something that everyone could enjoy went up. Something that would bring peace, solace, and happiness to many. So, we donated the land to the city as the site of the future Thomas Paige Library. We hope this will be a place that will better lives and not tear them apart. Thank you."

Sniffles abounded. Plenty of them. I handed a tissue to the woman to my left, my prep work coming in handy. But none of the sniffles were mine. I simply wasn't a crier, but I was definitely a stiff upper lipper. While I hadn't known Thomas Paige, I was glad to have played a part in finding and capturing everyone involved with his murder. Two important things stood out in the process: (1) justice had been served, and (2) life was short. So much shorter than it should be for some people.

"This was . . ." John trailed off as if he wasn't sure what to say, and I didn't know how to fill in the blank. Perhaps it was the uncharacteristic note of emotion in his voice that stumped me. The man was stoic, and with good reason. But right now, he seemed . . . not stoic as he said softly, "It's good to have closure."

As the lead detective on the Thomas Paige investigation, surely John needed the closure too, maybe in a different way than the Sloan family. In a way that gave him the drive to move on to solving the next crime.

I turned my focus back to Michael and the mayor as they went through the ceremony of breaking ground, Michael taking the shovel and spearing it into the earth and turning over a chunk of dirt. A bubble of tension popped, and the assembly broke into applause as the mayor shook Michael's hand and they both smiled for the flashing cameras.

"I'm not sure it's closure," I said, picking up where John left off, "since it feels like this library might open doors for people."

John regarded me sideways, as if deciding whether I was going for a pun or something deeper. "That was oddly profound for a Thursday morning."

I shrugged. "It's what I think."

He nodded, standing with his hands in his pockets, still thoughtful. Then our eyes met. "So do I. I feel the same. It's the kind of thing you hold on to so you can keep doing what you do, you know?"

I did know, and we both broke eye contact and turned, watching the people who had become as much family as they were friends pose for press photos, their smiles ranging from peaceful to bittersweet.

When we left, John walked me to my car, held the door open for me, and said goodbye. As I slid into the driver's seat, his gaze seemed to linger for a little longer than usual.

"You know, I was going to . . ."

Intrigued, I waited for him to finish. But then he shook his head.

"What is it?" I prodded. He wasn't seriously going to leave me wondering, was he?

"Nothing." He shook his head again. The frown unknotted from between his brows. "I'll see you at the gym." He gave me a smile and pushed my car door closed before hopping into his LEAF.

As I drove away, one thought played over and over in my mind. What was it that he hadn't allowed himself to say?

2

MINDY

The hostess didn't bother giving Brent and me menus anymore. We'd been meeting at the restaurant in the Luxe for breakfast for years. Even the new staff was used to us—especially Brent, since he worked in the hotel.

Food was good. Friendship was better. *Usually.*

"All right," Brent said, leaning back in the booth after the server had brought our drinks. "Tell me if I'm crazy, but did I detect a vibe between you and the detective yesterday?"

"At the groundbreaking?" I stared at him over my coffee mug. "You're crazy."

Brent broke into a grin that didn't bode well for my keep-it-under-wraps efforts. "What's so terrible about making flirty eyes with him at a groundbreaking ceremony, your majesty?" he asked. "Does it lack decorum? I proposed to my wife in a cemetery."

"Aw!" Covering my heart with my hands, I pretended to swoon. "You are so romantic!" I dropped my hands and the act. "Said no one ever."

Though I doubted that was true. Shannon, I bet, thought he was the most romantic. And he probably agreed with her.

"Also," I went on, "can I just point out the ridiculousness of using yourself as a model of decorum?"

He considered that for a moment. "Good point," he conceded, then leaned his elbows on the table. "Now, if you're done changing the subject, I'll ask again. Are you ever going to tell Detective John Winston how you're crushing on him, and that you write his name with little curlicue hearts in your notebook?"

I considered a range of tactics—denial, avoidance, change of subject. But why pick one when I could go with a cocktail mix? "You miss the stage, don't you? Your moments of stand-up? Have your fun, but let the record reflect those are lies." I stabbed the table with my finger. "Vicious lies. Because I'm not in middle school. I didn't do that back then, and I don't do it now."

"I bet you do." Brent leaned farther in. "It's just the kind of thing you'd do—scribble a note to your secret crush in your diary, then lock it up and hide the notebook under your bed."

I wanted to swat him with a pancake. Where was our food? "Brent," I said, more patiently than I felt. "I have three sisters. I'd have been an idiot to put anything in writing."

"Fair point," he said after a beat. Then he raised a not-so-fast finger. "But you live alone now. I'm not going to believe you until you show me your diary."

"Good luck with that, then, because, one, I don't have a diary, and two... *no*."

I was saved by the server arriving with our food, and we both sat back so she could put the plates on the table. I asked for a warm-up on my coffee, hoping that by the time she was done, Brent would have changed the subject. After all, John was damned attractive, but I'd had him inked in under "professional contacts." Or maybe "colleagues." Now that we worked out at the gym together, I'd say he'd stepped out of the "friend of a friend" column and into the "friend of mine" box, but he couldn't be anything more than that.

"Well, I think there's something there." He raised his eyebrows as he stabbed his pancake. "I could just see the two of you doing coupley things together. Going on dates to the movies, hands touching in the popcorn box. Dancing..."

"I do not dance." My cheeks burned, but in reality, I did. Dance, that was.

We'd danced at Sophie and Ryan's wedding. The two single people in a party full of couples.

Pairing off was inevitable. Unavoidable. And, quite simply, irresistible.

At least, that was my memory of the night. It still brought a flush to my skin, but I held on to every detail of dancing with John as Ella Fitzgerald had crooned "Let's Fall in Love."

3

MINDY

Several months ago

Everything about the wedding was wonderful, from the food to the music to the fit of the tux on the man who gave the bride away. He wore it well, and he still looked good later at the reception at Mandalay Bay. He also looked happy, and that was a good look on him too.

John and I were the only ones left at our table as the dancing started and coupled-up guests took to the floor. A few songs in, Ella Fitzgerald crooned, beckoning us.

"Want to take a spin?" John asked.

"Sure."

Once on the dance floor, he placed his arm around my waist and his hand clasped mine, his gaze intent and curious. Almost as if he was taking in all my features to remember later.

I never blushed, so the heat spreading from my chest and tingling to my fingertips had to be something else.

I didn't know what. Stranger still, I wasn't sure what to say, which was incredibly unlike me.

When the silence stretched longer than I could stand, I said, "You're a pretty good dancer."

"For a cop, you mean." He grinned.

"For anybody," I told him, laughing. "But you could use some work on accepting compliments."

"Let's turn it around, then." He still held my gaze, his blue eyes crinkling at the corners. "You have a lovely laugh."

"Thank you," I said softly, loving the sweet words, tucking them away someplace inside me so I could recall them later.

John didn't seem desperate to fill the silence, but it pushed hard on me, pointing out this was an opportunity I shouldn't waste. With the investigation into the Paige murder now closed, maybe this was what I'd hoped for—the chance to let John know I wanted to learn more about him. I needed to show I was interested in John Winston, the person. Because I was.

"So . . . you dance." I laugh. "What else do you do that defies expectations?"

He seemed to appreciate the question, giving

it some thought. "I'm a fan of classic crime fiction."

I narrowed my eyes playfully. "That doesn't really come as a surprise. You're a detective. Of course you identify with . . . who is it? Philip Marlowe? Sam Spade?"

"Sherlock Holmes."

"Hmm . . . duly noted."

He looked a little wary, but then I caught the glint of humor in his eyes. "Is it important, which one I identify with?"

"Not at all, which is, as Agatha Christie would say, what makes it so interesting."

"Ah, I see. You're a Miss Marple fan."

I shook my head. "No . . . I mean, yes, I love those stories, but if I had to pick, I like them hard-boiled. It's Dashiell Hammett and Raymond Chandler all the way."

"Hmm . . ." he said, echoing me. "That tracks."

I shot him a sharp stare. "Are you saying I'm hard-boiled?"

"No." He slowly trailed his studying gaze over my face, my blonde hair, to my shoulder. Finally, his gaze trailed along my collarbone. I could feel it like a feathering touch running up my neck to below my jaw. And I could feel, too, the depth of my wish that he'd trace a finger over my hair. "You look soft and goddamn—"

He broke off, and I held my breath. One beat, two beats . . .

They were fast, my heartbeats, and they were drowned out by the pounding rhythm coming from the speakers.

When had the music changed? And who'd put on "Mamma Mia"? Unacceptable—bring back Ella Fitzgerald, please. I hadn't even noticed that we'd stopped at the edge of the dance floor, out of the way of people getting their dance on, and out of the figurative spotlight.

What did I look soft and goddamn like?

"You can't leave me hanging like that, John," I said, almost as exasperated as I pretended to be.

He dropped his arm and released my hand but didn't step back. The wheels were clearly turning in his head, but I couldn't tell what he was thinking.

A waiter circled by with champagne.

John glanced at the tray but didn't take any.

"We should get . . . coffee sometime," he said, spinning me around with his sudden suggestion.

"Coffee?" I repeated. Had he meant to ask me for coffee? Because he'd been looking at the drinks tray. His voice *was* champagne.

"Yes, coffee."

We'd had coffee before. To talk about work. To trade theories on the investigation. The case was now closed, and his tone said *drinks*. But he'd definitely said the word "coffee"—twice.

And I wasn't one to lean on subtext.

He ran his hand over his hair like he was nervous, which was not a word I would have associated with John Winston. Then the awkwardness was gone, and he seemed to regain his footing. "Let me know when you're free."

4

MINDY

Perhaps I had lingered too long on that memory.

It was one of my favorites, despite how it had ended.

But now, at breakfast in the Luxe, I stirred cream into my coffee. And continued to stir.

Until Brent reached across the table and stilled my hand. "Mindy, stop. I give up. Just, please—I can't take one more clink of that spoon."

Apparently, I'd been stirring for a long time, lost in my thoughts. "Wait, what are you giving up?"

"Bugging you about your not-as-unrequited-as-you-think feelings for John."

With a huge sigh, I dropped my spoon on the table. "I'm telling you the truth, Brent. If something were going to happen between John and me, it would have already happened." I picked up my cup in both hands and sighed more softly. I was going to need another reheat. "We had a chance. After the Thomas Paige investigation finally wrapped up, we even set up an appointment for coffee."

"Coffee as in work-colleagues coffee or coffee as in a starter date?"

"Hard to say. The man is a bit inscrutable."

He shot me a look that spoke volumes. "And your talent is reading people."

"True. But I haven't mastered reading that man. If I were a betting woman, I'd say yes, it seemed like a *potential* date. But I don't like to assume. And maybe that's for the best. Because the maybe-date coffee never happened. John was called to a homicide and had to cancel. And then the next time, I had an emergency at work." I made a *and so on* gesture. Because so it went. "Then we started working out together, and now he's my sparring partner, and . . ." I shrugged. "This is where we've settled, and it works for us."

Brent frowned, but gently. "I think 'settled' is a telling word, Queen Mindy." The affectionate nickname took any sting out of the comment. "If you have time to be friends, you could make time to be more."

But did I? Could I? I wasn't so sure. I'd always trusted signs, and they all pointed to the fact that we were buddies. John and I were best that way. Besides, I didn't crave the same things my friends had in their lives. "Just because you're all married and popping out babies, doesn't mean everyone should be." I stared into my lukewarm coffee. "Not everyone is meant for that."

"I know." He held up his hands in surrender, but he was serious when he added, "But I worry about you."

I looked away. Truth was, sometimes I worried about me too.

Brent didn't dance around the topic, which was one reason we were friends, but he spoke gently. "I worry that you put your heart on ice when Cody died in Afghanistan."

My fiancé and I had been together for four years, engaged for one. He'd proposed when we both came back from deployment. I didn't reenlist when my time was up, but Cody went back for a second tour and was killed.

That was six years ago.

Brent wasn't wrong—I'd grieved hard, and, yes, it did feel as if the part of me that could love someone had died with Cody. But scars healed. I'd made it through, leaning on my friends and my job. Security work was not nearly as challenging as the military had been, but it was rewarding in its own way.

And it had provided a soft landing for me after Cody's death.

Now, six years later, I still had work to fall back on—such that it was right now—and my friends and my sisters. Plus, I had a sacred duty as book supplier for my nieces and nephews—the ones in Colorado and the new ones I'd unofficially adopted here.

"You say 'settled' like it's a bad thing," I said. "I know what you mean, but when you feel *un*settled—like you're in zero gravity and nothing is bolted down to hold on to—stability and consistency trump romantic drama."

Brent stared at me, looking dissatisfied with my answer and making sure I saw him looking dissatisfied with it. His eyebrow arch seemed to last a long time before he let it go. "Don't think we won't come back to that another time. But you just reminded me to ask how things are going at the Jade. It's been almost a year since you left the Wynn for the new gig. I'm sensing lately it's not all you'd hoped it would be."

"Understatement of the year." I leaned back in the booth, demonstrating how tired I was of the runaround. "My boss—"

I jerked my head up, making sure no one was in earshot. I even stretched up to look into the next booth. Las Vegas, especially the Strip, could be such a small world.

Satisfied we had a window of privacy, I went on, but didn't name names. "I always thought that buyouts by soulless new owners were a cliché. But here I am, working on a temporary contract in a job I've been doing for nearly eight years.

And there *they* are, stringing me along with the promise of a permanent job and benefits and a 401K. A 401K would go a long way toward making me feel more settled."

He tapped his fingers on the table. "No promises, but if you want, I could check around—"

"Nope." I held up my hands like double stop signs. "Do. Not. Want." At Brent's frown, I softened my tone. "Seriously, Brent. I don't want favors." I paused. "At least, not right now."

"What *do* you want right now?" he asked. "Besides a retirement plan?"

"I'd settle for a freaking hot cup of coffee."

And it came—the jolt of energy I needed for a nonstop day. The kind of day that invigorated me. That reminded me why I loved my job.

In spite of a classic sexist boss, I still loved every damn thing about this gig.

If only it came with a little more security.

When my boss called me into his office that evening, I sent a wish out to the universe that he'd finally offer me a permanent post.

But when I went in, the look on his face didn't suggest an offer was coming my way.

The look on his face said *you're fired*.

5

JOHN

From the first bark that echoed from inside the rundown building on the outskirts of town, *I knew*.

I saw it like I had a crystal ball or an enchanted mirror maybe—the magical power of knowing my sister well.

Sophie would go in and greet those working dogs with her heart pinned on her sleeve—because her heart was always on her sleeve—and lose it completely. And by "lose it," I meant hire a van, load up all the pooches, take them home with her, and bake them homemade biscuits for every meal.

On the one hand, that was a damn fine idea.

On the other, she'd have her hands full in a month with a baby, so it was best for someone to put the brakes on that.

I'd arrived first too, a few minutes ahead of

the hour—no gaming the navigation app today. Usually, a timely arrival meant a little breathing room before my sister showed up. But today, Sophie was uncharacteristically punctual.

And when her Aston Martin pulled into the lot, I knew why.

Ryan got out of the driver's seat, walked around, and opened the door for his wife. He kept time like an atomic clock.

I tipped my chin in his direction. "Nice ride."

"It's not too bad," he deadpanned. "Hope you don't mind my joining you two, but I can't help myself when it comes to dogs."

Huh. Maybe I'd have to run interference for him too.

He offered a hand to Sophie.

"I can get out of the car myself," she said, but she didn't refuse his help or hide that she was grateful for it.

"Oof," she muttered as she stood and stretched her back.

"I see pregnancy isn't slowing you down in the fashion department," I remarked, gesturing to her red dress with lemon slices for polka dots, pinup-style, as it always was with her. She'd simply adjusted the hemline.

Her face lit up. "That's another thing I love about pregnancy," she said. "It's a chance for a whole new wardrobe."

Ryan grinned—a sappy, blissed-out, proud-husband-and-future-father grin—and said, "That's my Sophie."

The three of us walked to the front door of the shelter. It was just one standard glass door lettered with the suite number and a sign above—K-9 BUDDIES. Not much else distinguished the place from the other doors of the industrial park except the yips and barks of dogs being dogs. I suspected there was a door open in the back of the building to let the breeze in and the sounds out. As I'd driven up, I'd spotted an overhang that shaded a clean but utilitarian dog run. It wasn't doggie nirvana, but this wasn't meant to be a long-term situation.

Nor did it invite the casual animal lover to drop in and look for a pet for little Timmy or Suzie either. These were retired working dogs—they'd need the right homes and the right handlers.

"Thank you again for coming with me," Sophie said, curling her hand around my arm as we went up the three steps to the door. "Having you and Ryan here will help immensely."

"Don't think twice about it." I covered her hand with my free one and squeezed. "I want to see every rescue dog in a happy home. But especially these doggos who've worked hard, dangerous jobs and deserve a retirement full of kibble and belly scratches."

Ryan made a choking sound, maybe a cough,

maybe a laugh. "Did you just say 'doggos'? No more social media for you, John."

I gave him an unperturbed look I'd honed since my days as a rookie. "When would I have time for social media?"

No one could argue with that. When did I have time for social anything?

I didn't get the word from a meme. Mindy had said it when our new running route took us past a dog park.

"Who's a good doggo?" she'd singsonged to the stocky Labrador retriever who'd recognized a sucker when he saw one. He was missing a front leg, but that hadn't stopped him from barreling into Mindy and begging for attention.

"Aren't you a sweet doggo?" she'd asked. "No, I don't have treats, but I'll give you all the nose boops. Yes, I will."

The three-legged dog was a curiosity, but so was Mindy. Who was this woman holding the dog's head between her hands as he grinned at her? I didn't blame him. I'd be pretty pleased if she grabbed the hair behind my ears too.

I knew she loved animals, but I didn't expect so much cooing and cajoling. Mindy was personable and professional, and I'd appreciated both those qualities from the moment we met. I had been deep in an investigation, and admittedly, I'd viewed her through that lens at first. She'd offered her help, something that, as a detective, pinged my radar. I'd quickly realized that was in character for her. She had connections, and she could tap into information that would take the LVPD twice the time and effort to get. Why risk burning an undercover officer or an informant when Mindy had cultivated resources over her eight years working in hotel security?

The woman was head-turning, drop-dead beautiful. On top of that, she was self-sufficient and capable, and the whole package was straight-up sexy as hell.

And when she let loose, she could kick the shit out of a heavy bag. She never pulled her punches when we sparred. When she jabbed, she let loose a warrior yell that haunted my dreams. I often laid awake thinking about what sounds she might make for me if she were in my bed beside me.

And now, after the dog park, I had a whole new library of squeals and croons and flirty sounds to imagine.

But I didn't need to be imagining them now.

Sophie patted my arm before she let go. "I'm grateful in any case. You and Ryan can offer a different perspective than mine, and I think the organizers will appreciate your . . . vibe."

This time when I glanced at my brother-in-law it was for clarification. "She means our alpha manliness," Ryan explained.

"Obviously," I agreed.

"I don't *not* mean that," Sophie teased her husband. "But more that you work in law enforcement and security."

Determined to work until she popped, Sophie had one last fundraiser to spearhead, this one for a locally based organization that found homes for working dogs—former military or police dogs. I'd never had a K-9 partner, but I'd worked with the teams on the force who did. It was a cause near and dear to my heart.

I was a dog lover, and I wanted those dogs to have a good home after serving their community or country. But they needed the *right* home, and that took resources.

Ryan employed several dog-and-handler teams at his security firm, so he had a similar interest and appreciation as mine. We also had similar resources, which might be needed if it came to tracking down a former handler, for example. Often, K-9 teams were split up by deployments in the military, and the former handlers still had room in their hearts for a *doggo* friend.

I held the door for my sister, and Ryan and I followed her inside. The room was sparse—only an unoccupied reception desk, a worn-out sofa, and a wall full of pictures of rescued dogs and their new owners filled the space. *Heartwarming* didn't cover it.

"Oh, I have so many ideas for this fundraiser."

Sophie clapped her hands together while we waited for her appointment. "John, I'm really glad you discovered this organization."

"Not me." I didn't want to take someone else's credit. "That was Mindy and Sergeant Jackson in the dog park."

Sophie perked up with interest. "Sergeant Jackson is the three-legged dog?"

"That's him." The good doggo's owner, Matthew, had told us about the organization. Like his dog, Matthew was missing a leg. It had come up in our conversation about Sergeant Jackson, and how he'd been an explosive-detecting K-9 until he'd been injured by an IED—the same way Matthew had lost his.

"Fate," the man had said, rubbing the dog's head. "I needed a running partner who could pace me."

I'd watched Mindy carefully as she'd laughed and shared with Matthew stories of their time in the military, tales no one else could really understand.

I knew her fiancé had been killed in the Middle East, but if there were shadows in her thoughts just then, they didn't show. She'd seemed relaxed, like Matthew and Sergeant Jackson's contentment had rubbed off on her.

I didn't want to miss an opportunity, so I'd asked him for the name and number of the organization that had matched him and Sergeant

Jackson. I tried not to bring projects to Sophie too often, not wanting to take advantage. Or saving my markers for when it counted maybe.

When he'd tapped the info into my phone, Mindy had looked at the two of us like her heart was growing bigger in her chest in that very moment.

Well, dogs did know the way to one's heart.

"Anyway," said Sophie, "we need to make sure that Sergeant Jackson and his new family come to the fundraiser. I hope everyone will be as excited about it as I am."

"I can't see how they won't," I said. "You specialize in getting people excited about something, right? Especially about opening their wallets."

"Well, I don't take on a cause unless I believe in it," she protested.

I raised my hands in surrender. "I didn't mean anything bad by it. Only good. This is a good reason to open your wallet."

"I couldn't agree more," she said.

Ryan sunk onto the battered sofa and patted the cushion beside him. "Come and get off your feet, Sophie."

But my sister was, appropriately, like a terrier following a scent. And she was studying me. "Since we have a minute, I'll tell you what other cause is on my radar."

"Look out," murmured Ryan.

Now I was worried.

Sophie rubbed her palms together. "Let's talk about my idea for you, dear brother."

"Me?" I pointed at my chest, as if she could mean anyone else.

"Yes. I know I'm not a detective, but I can put two and two together," she said.

Ryan chuckled. "Yeah, because the clues are pretty obvious."

I furrowed my brow. "What are you talking about?"

With a tsk, she pursed her lips like I was the one being stubborn. "As if you don't know."

I glanced at Ryan, who gave me no help, then back at my sister. "I swear I have no idea what you're talking about."

She parked a hand on her hip, which was amusing, given the size of her, but I didn't dare laugh. "That whole 'Mindy and the dog' story." She took a beat, her gaze locking firmly on me. "John Henry Winston. I'm talking about you and Mindy."

"What about Mindy and me?" I asked in my most neutral voice. It came easily, since I used it all the time at work.

And other times too.

At work, the mask was a tool. A way to stay in control of an interview or interrogation. Even a confrontation.

Outside of work, it was habit—or it had been

until Mindy, when it had become more like camouflage.

And I had no idea whether Mindy could see through it or not. Sometimes I thought so, that she glimpsed something of the tangled emotions she evoked in me, the rare moment of indecision. And sometimes I wondered if she only saw the workaholic, single-minded detective. She wouldn't be entirely wrong on that count.

Sophie rolled her eyes. "Look, I'm eight months pregnant and that gives me permission to say anything I want. Wait—actually, I would tell you this even if I wasn't pregnant." She wagged a finger under my nose. "You need to do something about all that chemistry between you two."

"The what?"

"I was dead sure at our wedding that the two of you were finally going to take care of business." She shook her head. "But all these months later, you two are still throwing off sparks."

"You kind of do, man," Ryan chimed in.

I shook my head in denial. "I don't know what you're talking about. You're mistaking camaraderie for chemistry."

That was such a lie. I'd felt sparks from the second I met Mindy a year ago at Sophie and Ryan's engagement party at New York–New York.

Her eyes had drawn me in, but so had her spitfire personality. She'd been bold and friendly, not waiting for an introduction before launching into a proposition. I'd been in the thick of the Thomas Paige investigation, and she'd offered to help in any way she could.

That case was exactly why I'd had to tamp down the instant attraction I felt for her. I wasn't going to risk compromising one of the most important cases I'd ever worked on. Not with a distraction or anything else.

Hell, all active cases were the most important, taking priority over home, hobbies, and especially relationships.

So I'd shoved that lust for Mindy into a box and set it aside.

But desire was desire, and sometimes it was a force of its own. Like the time it had cropped up again at Sophie's wedding and I'd wanted so damn badly to ask her out for drinks.

No, that wasn't honest. I'd wanted so damn badly to kiss her, to wrap her hair around my hand and not let her go until her knees wobbled. Asking her out for drinks would have been a first step.

But I hadn't. What had come out was "coffee," like my tongue thought it knew better than the rest of me.

Ah, one of my life's regrets.

Heavy footsteps came down the hall from the back of the building, and a man poked his head into the front office. "Sorry to keep you waiting.

When I get Army brass on the phone, I have to get through all my talking points before I hang up, because it may be a while before I can manage such a feat again."

"I understand," Sophie said graciously. "Thanks for taking the time to meet with us."

"Not at all. It's you who's doing us the favor, Mrs. Sloan." He looked from her to Ryan—who'd stood up—to me, and Sophie introduced us.

"Randall Parks," the man said, with a firm handshake and good eye contact. "So . . . you want to go back and meet some of the dogs?"

"Absolutely!" Her answer was instantaneous. Proof that dog people can recognize one another, obviously.

Parks led the way, and Ryan followed along with Sophie. But my sister stopped at the door, turning and stopping me with a hand on my chest. "You're off the hook for now, brother mine," she said breezily. "Because . . . dogs. But I'll just say this—life is short, as you know. Maybe just . . . go for it."

Ryan had paused to wait for her, so she hurried to catch up with him, leaving me to bring up the rear.

It allowed me to think without my sister's eagle eye watching my expression for any clue as to what I was thinking or feeling. But if she could figure that out, she'd be ahead of me.

So my thoughts went to what was in front of

me. The narrow warehouse space was ample for the dogs here—and ample enough to demonstrate that an apartment would be a terrible fit, no pun intended, for an animal used to productive activity. Some kept playing, a few came to check us out, and a few hung out, content where they were. But they all reminded me of kids let out of class for recess.

These dogs needed a whole lot more.

More than a handler or a partner. They needed a home. A family. I'd had partners and colleagues. I had Sophie and now the Sloans. But it wasn't quite the same thing as the safe landing spot of someone who could welcome you into their arms and vice versa.

I was a long way from retiring, and I hoped that it wouldn't be forced on me by some circumstance. But when I looked at these hardworking dogs enjoying their downtime, I understood where their joy came from. It wasn't just because they were off duty, or off the leash, or free to roam. It was because they weren't alone.

For so long, the Sloan case had dominated my waking hours, been my constant companion. When it wrapped, my off-duty hours seemed lonely. My condo felt vacant. But then there was Mindy, making inroads into my downtime and sliding into my thoughts.

In the past year, I'd realized that work occupied space but didn't fill up a life.

It didn't take Sherlock Holmes to deduce that a romance with Mindy would be incredible. But the next big case would come along and push out everything else. I'd been there before. I didn't want Mindy to get frustrated and resentful and storm out of my life completely, didn't want her to think I didn't care about her.

But could I play it safe and stay alone forever? Maybe Sophie was right that it was time to take a chance.

I had to think about what mattered most later.

At the moment, it was time to focus on one particular mission: saving Sophie and Ryan from themselves.

Because they were both telling Randall they wanted to take home Ajax the beagle, Radar the Malinois, and Holmes the shepherd.

"Just one, guys," I said, stepping in. "Just one."

6

MINDY

I stared at Jensen, my boss, such that he was.

Emphasis on "was."

He'd already turned to face his computer, clicking fast, like he was ticking boxes on a form inquiring about his hobbies:

✔ Be an entitled asshole at the breakfast buffet.

✔ Misappropriate security cameras to scope out attractive women losing money and feeling vulnerable.

✔ Ruin someone's life.

"You're firing me?" He hadn't been ambiguous about it, but I still needed to make sure this wasn't a nightmare.

"No," said Jensen, with a bark and an eye roll. "As a contractor, you were never technically hired. Ergo, you can't be fired."

What kind of douchebag says "ergo" when they're giving someone the ax?

All right, that shouldn't have been a surprise. If asked that question ten minutes ago, I would have pointed at Jensen for my answer. *That* kind of douchebag.

But the firing—excuse me, the termination of my contract—came out of the blue. Sure, things had been stressful lately, with bad hours and unreasonable demands, but I'd just thought that was Jensen being Jensen.

"But . . . I left the Wynn for this position." I sounded stunned, which I was, and defeated, which I was not. Even if he was a douche, I didn't want to lose a job that I mostly loved. I sat up straight, ready to make my case. "The Jade came to me. Management promised me matching funds and a 401K."

A careless shrug came my way, then a dismissive "Sorry, sweetheart. The old management recruited you. The new ownership has decided it's time to bring in its own people."

"So you're going too?" Was I mean enough to find satisfaction in that?

I remembered how he'd called me "sweetheart" and "babe" and "honey" whenever he could get away with it, and I decided that yes, I was that mean.

Jensen spun his chair around and grabbed some paper from the printer, tapped it on the desk, and stapled it. "Nope. Because *my* contract specifies the penalty they'd have to pay to terminate it early. Always read the fine print, doll face." He handed the packet over the desk with a sharky smile I wanted to punch off his face. "Now, take that to HR, and don't forget that your nondisclosure remains in effect, so no talking about the buyout to anyone. Just tell your friends you're taking some 'me time' or whatever you girls do." He waved a hand as if he were talking about periods, and it was just too much.

I snatched the papers from him, and he yelped.

Oops. My bad. *Not.*

Collateral damage? His paper cut.

He sucked his cut finger as I suppressed a smile.

"Is that all?" I asked coldly.

"Yeah. Don't forget to leave your keys after you clean out your office." He picked up a pencil and tapped it on the desk. "Nothing personal, sweet cheeks. Come back and visit the Jade any time, and please keep us in mind if you have guests coming to town or need to host an event."

"Nothing personal, Jensen," I said, opening the door to let myself out, "but I hope you get lemon juice in your paper cut." Then I stopped, stared at him, and said, "Also, don't call me 'doll face,' 'sweet cheeks,' 'honey,' or 'babe' ever again."

* * *

I only needed a handful of minutes to grab the pictures of my nieces and nephew from my desk and make sure I hadn't left anything in the drawers. I'd never kept much in there but a few protein bars and some emergency tampons. My job hadn't been to sit at a desk. It was to put out fires—usually figurative—or to prevent them by keeping my eyes and ears open and staying one step ahead. How sad to have been blindsided by my own firing.

I'd never been fired.

What was I supposed to do? What did this mean? And was it somehow my fault?

Grabbing my phone, I dialed Lynette, my oldest sister. Between her and my brother-in-law, one of them must have lost a job abruptly. I needed someone to walk me through this, or maybe simply to tell me I wasn't a loser.

Lynette answered on the third ring in a whispering hiss. "Mindy! You called."

That was a strangely obvious observation. "Where are you?"

"PTA meeting," she whispered. "Are you okay?"

Ohhh. Now I understood her surprise and worry. Lynette's twins were preteens, and nothing short of the apocalypse rated more than a text.

"Yes," I assured her. "Well, nothing that involves stitches or X-rays."

"I'm so glad. Can I call you back later?"

"Sure. I don't want you to get in deep with the PTA."

"You probably have mafia dons in Las Vegas who I'd rather piss off more than the PTA. Talk to you later."

I smiled. I'd stake one of those gluten-free granola-eating soccer moms against any mafioso godfather.

But allowing for the time-zone difference and her kids' schedules, I didn't hold out on her calling back tonight. If I had asked, she would have stepped out of the meeting or told the boys to eat cereal for dinner while she talked to Aunt Mindy. But why throw everyone out of whack? Presumably, I'd still be unemployed tomorrow.

I took my work keys off my key ring and gave them to Jensen's assistant, who was supposed to be *our* assistant, but he bogarted all her time. She gave me a hug, assured me not to worry about her—she already had a line on a new job—and mentioned staying in touch, which I doubted but appreciated the thought.

My stomach growled, and I sighed. Maybe I had time to grab something in one of the Jade's restaurants before anyone knew better than to give me the employee discount.

Shouldering my purse, I headed that way,

weaving through the maze of singing slot machines and debating whether to call one of my other sisters. But their kids were younger, so they might be in the middle of bath and bedtime. I could text Brent, but he'd probably be in the same situation with his kiddo. Like Lynette, he'd make time to talk if I asked for it, but I didn't want to be the person texting with drama.

That wasn't my jam.

Funny. I'd never worried before what I would do in a big emergency, never doubting my friends and family would pull off a miracle for me if they had to. But keeping the day-to-day things—asshole bosses, car trouble, paper cuts—to myself doubled the lonely factor.

Too bad most of life was made up of the latter.

Though my thoughts were turned inward, my senses were tuned outward, because only the most naive tourists didn't watch where they were going in a casino. My gaze snagged on a familiar couple before they spotted me—a willowy redhead holding hands with her tall, dark, and objectively handsome husband.

"Annalise! Michael!" I shouted with joy, like I hadn't seen them in ages. They broke into twin smiles when they saw me flagging them down like an air traffic controller.

"Hey, Mindy. Good to see you," Michael said, with Annalise adding, "You look fabulous."

I didn't feel fabulous, but I was grateful nonetheless.

My exuberance seemed out of proportion to the run-in, but it went with my out-of-proportion relief at seeing a pair of familiar faces. "You're here!" It seemed I was taking a page from Lynette's book and stating the obvious. "I mean, in Vegas." I groaned silently and collected my scattered thoughts and emotions. "Also, I mean in the Jade, like a couple of conventioneers." Taking a breath, I tried one more time. "I mean, I didn't expect to see you, but it's good to see you."

"You took the words right out of my mouth. We were on our way to have dinner here and thought we'd find you and see if you wanted to join us." Annalise kissed one cheek and the other, very continental, then gave me a proper American hug.

Michael smiled at his wife. He'd pined for the woman for eighteen years—until they reunited a little more than a year ago. Now, he was in mad love with her, and the look he gave her . . . For a moment, that rootless feeling gnawed at me again, and I longed for even a morsel of what they had.

He turned back to me. "What do you say, Gamble? Sushi at the Jade? The rainbow rolls are the best on the Strip, as someone once told me."

He winked. That someone was me.

But in a heartbeat, all my out-of-place exuberance drained.

And I knew the answer to how it felt to lose a job. Flustered, mad, emotional, and like you wanted to cling to the familiar.

My emotions plummeted from the sky to the floor as I blurted, "Good thing you came tonight, then, since it's my last day working here."

"What's this?" Annalise asked in surprise. "I know the Jade wasn't all you'd hoped it would be. Have you decided to move on?"

My hum was ambiguous. I'd rather have let them go on and enjoy their dinner and not dump my drama on them, but I also didn't want to hide the truth from my friends. I needed to let it out. "It wasn't really my decision. Business politics, you know."

Michael, frowning, nodded. "I hear you. Our industry has seen its fair share of revolving doors these days." His tone was sympathetic—he may have been contemplating troubles of his own. He and Ryan ran a private security firm, and he knew how the merry-go-round of politics in our industry spun.

"What are you going to do? Want to talk about it over sake and edamame?" Annalise asked, tipping her forehead toward the sushi joint I loved.

Briefly tempted to join them, I took a step in that direction.

Then I stopped. "Actually, I am going to let you two enjoy your dinner." I gave her another hug. "You can help me strategize later."

"If you're sure?" she asked.

"I'm sure." Not only did the confidentiality agreement keep me from sharing in any detail, but I didn't want to presume on our friendship that way.

Because when I pictured myself leaning on a friend's shoulder, it was someone else I had in mind.

Someone I couldn't stop thinking of.

He was the one I needed right now.

* * *

After I sent Michael and Annalise on their way, I took out my phone, starting a text.

Mindy: I could use a drink.

Mindy: And by "drink," I mean a magic elixir that numbs your brain when you just found out you lost your job.

John: The hell? What moron would let you go from your job?

Mindy: Jensen.

John: Oh. Well. That's the moron, then. What's the reason?

Mindy: Do douchebags need a reason?

John: They never seem to.

Mindy: Besides, I wasn't fired. My contract was terminated.

John: What a douchebag.

Mindy: Right?!? Maybe I don't need a drink. Maybe I need to punch something.

John: Don't text anything that can be used in court to show intent.

Mindy: What am I, new?

John: Okay, don't text ME anything that would oblige me to interfere.

Mindy: I would never do that to you.

John: I know. I was joking.

Mindy: I don't know if that's sweet of you to say or sad for you that I couldn't tell.

John: Pretty sure it can be both.

Mindy: Wait. Are you saying you know I wouldn't do anything illegal or just that you trust me not to tell you about it?

John: . . .

Mindy: John?

John: Meet me at the gym in thirty.

Mindy: Make it forty. I have to change clothes.

As I re-read his texts, I caught myself almost smiling.

But not because of John.

Well, maybe a little because of John.

Because his humor—dry as it was—proved the world wasn't ending simply because I'd lost my job. The people in my life were the same as they were yesterday, would treat me the same way they always had.

Pensively, I scrolled through the exchange, then up to the messages before them. Genial. Supportive. Friendly.

Consistency is good, I reminded myself sternly. I

wouldn't be happy with anyone whose feelings turned on a dime.

God knew I was consistent—still longing for the same guy, no matter how many signs pointed to us staying just friends.

Like the fact that we were gym partners.

That screamed *be my friend*.

It didn't whisper *be my lover*.

Tonight, I needed the friend, but I wanted a little of both.

7

JOHN

Mindy's eyes narrowed, lasering in on the punching bag. "This is for calling me 'doll face.'" She turned her body, angled her hips, and flicked a kick at the heavy bag. Mad as she was, she still had great form.

Objectively speaking.

Subjectively too.

I was pretty sure there was a rule against asking a woman out within four hours of her losing her job. If not, there should be.

I'd have to table those plans, no matter how much I'd wanted to seize the moment earlier today. No matter how ready I finally was to level up from coffee to drinks to maybe a whole lot more.

And no matter how damn sexy the woman looked taking out her anger on the bag. There was just something hot as sin about a woman who knew how to channel her frustration into the physical.

And that had me wondering about other ways she might want to work off her frustration.

Ways I'd like to help.

But Mindy had more punches in her.

And I was smart enough not to start sparring until she'd taken some of her anger out on the literal punching bag. Just steadying the bag for her was workout enough.

She bounced on her toes, her blonde ponytail bobbing as she shifted her weight. "And this is for enjoying it so much."

Jab, jab, jab. Hook. Jab, jab, and . . . *kick*.

Oof. I felt that last one through the seventy-pound bag.

Perhaps that final kick did the trick, because she lowered her guard and shook out her hands, pacing now.

"Feeling better?" I asked.

"Much. Better. I needed that. Oh hell, did I need that."

I surveyed her up and down, taking stock—her breath was coming in a rush. Her chest was heaving. Her eyes were wild. "You look . . . good."

Fuck.

That came out all wrong.

Or rather, it came out *too* right. Too direct.

Too crystal clear. "Better, I meant." I backpedaled because . . . four-hour rule, right. "Like you feel more like yourself?"

She looked at me like I'd switched to speaking Swedish.

Goddammit.

I had a well-practiced poker face, but it required firing up my brain before my mouth.

I blamed Sophie. I'd been sparring with Mindy for nearly a year, keeping my thoughts on the straight and narrow, even when it took some willpower. Because when it came down to it, I'd rather have a successful friendship with her than an unsuccessful romance.

I didn't cross boundaries I set for myself. Not even in the gym when she wore those tops that made it impossible to tell if they were a bra or a shirt.

That was what she was wearing tonight, and it didn't help my resolve to be her shoulder to lean on.

She was flushed to a rosy glow and sweating the sexiest sweat a woman had ever sweated. It was like someone had opened all the blinds and I couldn't ignore the sunlight anymore.

"I do feel better," she answered.

"Want to spar a bit?" I asked, hoping it might keep my thoughts in line if she was trying to knock my block off.

"You sure?" She cocked an eyebrow. "You wussed out earlier."

"I did not wuss out. I didn't want to get my head caved in as a stand-in for your boss."

"Aw, it's sweet that you think I could dent your thick skull, Detective."

"Money where your mouth is, Ms. Gamble."

Working defense while Mindy let out more of her angst kept me focused where I should be. We maintained a comfortable silence as she set a slow, deliberate pace. I could tell she was thinking about something other than her strike placement but didn't ask what.

"Maybe this is a sign," she said as she edged up her speed. "Sometimes you need something to shake up the status quo."

She tried to sneak a hook in, but I blocked it. "But the hotel let you go because of a regime change," I pointed out. She'd sworn me to secrecy then explained about the buyout. "Not for a weakness or anything you can control."

"Not that." She threw a flurry of quick strikes against the pads on my hands. "But work is the only stable thing in my life. Or was."

"How can that be true? You have friends and family who aren't going to abandon you."

"I know." With a sigh, she lowered her hands and straightened from her fighting crouch. "But, John . . ." Her voice was more vulnerable than I'd ever heard it, and those two words, the sound of my name like that, dug into me and took root. "When Jensen dropped that bomb, it felt like he'd ripped the floor out from under me. I was mad, sure, but I was also really scared."

All my instincts told me to wrap her in my arms, to pull her tight for a hug. But I couldn't swear I could keep all touching friendly. It would be a dick move to make a move while she was so vulnerable.

"I can understand how that would knock you for a loop." Work took all my time, sometimes all my energy, but my job was part of my identity, private and public. "I'd feel adrift if I suddenly wasn't a detective."

"That's exactly how I'd describe it." She pulled off one of her gloves, signaling she was done for the night. "So, I think it's time to make some changes."

I blinked, surprised. "What kind of changes?" I was fine with change; I just liked enough warning to prevent it from happening, especially if it involved Mindy.

"The don't-put-all-my-eggs-in-one-basket kind, I guess." She shrugged and turned away to put her gloves in her gym bag. "And I hate that I don't get to see my sisters and their kids very often. I could move back to Colorado."

Shit. That was a terrible idea. No way could I let that happen. "But you hate the snow."

She shuddered, even in the heat of the gym. "True. I do. I despise the snow."

"There's a lot of snow in Colorado," I said leadingly.

Her eyes glinted with laughter. "That's some brilliant detective work, Winston."

"That's why they pay me the big bucks," I deadpanned. But she didn't say anything else about Colorado, so I could breathe again. Breathe and think more tactically.

Throwing the last of my gear in my gym bag, I picked it up and reached for hers too. "You want a life outside of work, right? Then you should talk to Sophie about the fundraiser she's doing."

"John . . ." She started to protest my carrying her bag, but then redirected. "First of all, you live in a glass house when it comes to work-life balance. Second, charity galas are really not my scene."

"Hear me out," I said. "Remember the three-legged dog from the park?"

"Sergeant Jackson? Of course I do."

I opened the door and gestured her ahead of me, thinking fast. Sophie wanted to play matchmaker, and Mindy wanted a life outside of work. A satisfying project while she weighed her options might show her what Las Vegas still had to offer her. Besides me.

"The charity that matched Sergeant Jackson with his new owner—that's who the event will benefit. Maybe you could be a volunteer. It's everything you like. It's going to be outside with a picnic and, I don't know, a dog costume contest or something."

"Um, is that dogs in costume or people costumed as dogs?" she asked.

"Does it matter?"

"Says the man who's never had to provide security during a furries convention."

"On the spectrum of out-of-towner shenanigans, dressing as cartoon animals for a weekend ranks pretty low."

She arched her brow. "Do you know how much it costs to repair a pool filter clogged with fun fur?"

We'd reached her car. "I'm torn between laughing and wondering how the hell we ended up talking about goddamn furries."

"Who says you have to choose only one?" she asked with a grin that was cheeky as hell.

And fuck it. She was right. Friendship, dating, work—I didn't know how long this quiet spell would last, but I had the chance to choose D, all of the above. Maybe I should take it as a gift and just enjoy it.

She unlocked her car and opened the door, holding out her hand for her gym bag. I gave her the strap but didn't let go yet.

Because I didn't want her to think of Colorado. I didn't want her to think of making big changes now. I wanted her to think of . . . well, of an *us*. I saw a work-around for the four-hours-after-firing rule, and I went for it. "Remember the other morning? At your car? When I said I wanted to ask you something?"

Her eyes widened, and her beautiful mouth opened in surprise. I watched the thoughts cross her face, flashing in tiny tics of emotion, refusing to settle into just one. "Yes," she finally said. "But you never finished the sentence."

Her words were soft, spoken in that vulnerable tone that was having its way with me tonight. And she was right. I hadn't gotten far before caution got the better of me.

Caution could go fuck itself.

Well, in this one area.

This area where I had nothing, and everything, to lose.

"Here's what I wanted to ask," I said. "Would you have a drink with me tomorrow night?"

After all the time I'd known her, I'd done it.

Asked her.

And I hoped she'd say yes.

But first, she tilted her head and shot me a quizzical stare.

"Is this because you feel sorry for me?"

"No." My swift answer left no space for doubt. "It's because I want to have a drink with you."

I took back her gym bag and leaned in to toss it onto the passenger seat, brushing up against her as I did, and not by accident. The little catch in her breath promised I wasn't alone in how I felt.

I straightened with one hand on the door and one on top of the car, letting my eyes travel over her lovely face. "I don't feel sorry for you, Mindy. You weren't happy at that job, and now you'll find a better one."

She shook her head. "So, the drinks—if they're not for commiseration, then they're for . . .?"

Ah, hell.

By now, it had to have been over four hours since she was fired.

"The drinks are for this." I leaned in and tucked a strand of hair over her ear. Then I dipped my head close to hers and brushed my lips against her cheek.

I stayed like that for a few seconds. Closer to her than I'd ever been. Wanting to be so much closer.

But I needed to be sure she was on the same page I was when it came to turning our friendship into something more.

That I wasn't taking advantage of her.

I pulled away. "What do you say?"

She licked her lips. "I say yes."

Stepping back, I waited until she'd buckled up and started the engine before heading to my own vehicle. This was good. This felt right. This was something I'd wanted for ages.

If getting together was a disaster, at least I'd know.

But with the way her eyes had darkened when I'd touched her hair, the way her breath came faster when I kissed her cheek?

This wasn't going to be a disaster at all.

8

MINDY

I couldn't remember the last time I'd been so excited for a date.

Okay, actually, I couldn't remember my last date, period.

But that wasn't the point.

The point was that John was taking me out for drinks—not for coffee, not for beers at a sports bar—but *drinks* and everything that implied. Drinks with my gorgeous, smart, sexy friend who was no longer locked in the friend zone.

If I'd had any doubts, John had put the remaining ones to rest with the way he'd said good night, his breath warm on my neck, his mouth skimming my jaw, leaving me wanting more, more, more.

As P!nk blasted in my condo—my Sexy Getting Ready Playlist, I'd dubbed it—I zipped up my jeans, slid on a silky top, and clasped on a slim silver pendant with a dog on it, a gift from my niece. Well, a dog *was* my Patronus, so it seemed fitting. Maybe it was also a sign that I *should* get involved with the dog rescue event. I'd worked with plenty of dogs in security.

I played out the possibilities as I swiped on some mascara, touched up my lip gloss, and sung my heart out to "Just Give Me a Reason."

I should *not* be this buoyant the day after getting canned.

But I was. Because . . . that *man*.

As the song faded out, my phone rang, and I jumped. I stared at the cell lit up on the bed, and hoped against hope that it wasn't John calling to cancel. Hoped no one had gotten murdered. Hoped tonight's plans weren't too good to be true.

Only one way to find out.

I swiveled around, marched to my bed, and grabbed the device, daring it to ruin my evening.

But John's name wasn't flashing across the screen. It was a number I didn't recognize, with a New York City area code.

Like most people, I didn't like answering unknown numbers, but neither the hotel business nor the security industry had nine-to-five hours, so I never ruled out it being something important, no matter the time of day.

"Mindy Gamble here."

"Hello, Ms. Gamble. This is Rosemary Adler at the Cartwright Hotel in New York." The woman on the other end of the call had a warm, confident tone. "I know this might seem out of the blue—well, not just seem so, it is—but for some time, we have been looking to fill the position of head of security here at our Manhattan property."

"Oh?" My heart sped up before I'd fully processed this information. New York had always seemed to me like a city where anything could happen, but on a less tawdry level than Las Vegas. "I hadn't heard."

"We've been selective with advertising the position, as we really want a certain kind of candidate." I could sense the smile in the voice on the other end of the call. "Which is why I'm calling. Our CEO has a friend who works at the Jade, and he passed on the fact that you might be searching for new employment."

I sat on the end of my bed. That was fast. Damned fast. Scary damned fast, in the way that a roller coaster operates at racetrack speeds. The this-is-thrilling-but-what-if-it-goes-horribly-wrong way.

"As it happens, Ms. Adler," I told her, "I am."

"Terrific. You have an excellent reputation in the industry. Do you have a few minutes to answer some preliminary interview questions?"

I blanched, checking the time on my nightstand clock. "Right now?" Ugh. I was already falling flat in the *brilliant answers* department.

"Yes. If that's okay," she said, giving me an out. But I needed to be *in* if I wanted to seize this opportunity.

And honestly, I did. I *had* to. It was perfect.

The Cartwright had an excellent reputation, and such a high-profile job at the New York site would be quite the gold star on my résumé.

Sure, the call had come out of the blue—well, so was my firing. And hadn't I just said I wanted a change? I'd been thinking Colorado, not the East Coast, but still.

If I was going to shake out the rug of my life, maybe I should go all in. Go for the scary roller coaster and not just the merry-go-round. I wouldn't know anyone in New York, but there was Skype, and there were frequent-flier programs. And there, I wouldn't be running in place while my friends forged ahead into new life stages. My whole life could be a new venture.

Also, I *did* have time to chat, because I was ready early. I just needed to slip on my shoes, which I did as I moved to a more businesslike place than my bed, settling into a chair at the kitchen table.

"This is fine, Ms. Adler," I said with impressive —I hoped—composure. "And I'd love to answer your questions."

* * *

The sign beckoned in flashes of '50s-style neon.

The Purple Zebra was off the Strip, a bar known mostly to locals, and it wasn't *crawling with Columbos*. That was how John had put it when he'd texted me the info earlier, which I took to mean it wasn't a cop hangout, or maybe just that it was free from other detectives who would buttonhole him with "just one more thing."

It was a perfect spot to talk. To swap stories. Maybe to have a heart-to-heart.

As much as I wanted to fast-forward to whispering sweet nothings—and, oh yes, I did want that—I also was bursting to share my news.

As I opened the door to the bar, I took an inventory of my emotional state, which had been doing a good imitation of a pendulum for the last twenty-four hours. Tonight, I was excited and nervous, and nervous and excited.

But as soon as I stepped inside, scanned the room, and spotted him, I was simply ready.

Ready for my date with the sexiest police officer in Las Vegas.

I'd seen him in gym clothes, in plain clothes, in a suit. Tonight, though, was my new favorite look on John Winston—dark jeans and a storm-cloud-gray Henley that hugged his chest in all the right places. Dear God, did it ever show off his biceps as he rose and walked toward me, his eyes on mine the whole damn time.

The hungry way he stared at me sent a shiver down my spine.

He set a hand on my arm and brushed my cheek with a kiss.

Who knew my cheek was an erogenous zone? It must have been, the way this man turned me on with the simplest of kisses.

"You look amazing," he said.

That word.

It was tossed about until it didn't mean much. It could describe that sandwich, this hairstyle, that nail color.

But from John, that word felt wholly real and powerful, and a little bit dirty too.

Which I liked.

"So do you." I wasn't prepared for how good it would feel to say that aloud. To finally give voice to all the attraction that had been bubbling for months.

For more than a year.

He set a hand on my back. It felt possessive as he walked me to a booth and gestured for me to sit down.

None of this was strange to me. I understood restaurant booths and was familiar with manners, had even experienced them in similar situations.

But not with John. This felt like a whole new side of him.

A part of him he was letting me see at last. That he wanted me to see.

He didn't want to be John, the kickboxing buddy.

He wanted to be John, the man I was going home with.

Because I was sure that was where this night was headed.

"Martini?" he asked.

"That sounds perfect," I said. "Especially since I have exciting news."

He lifted a brow in curiosity. "Martinis go well with news. Good news, I trust?"

"I think so."

He signaled the bartender, placed our order, then turned to me and prompted, "So..."

"I got the craziest call about an hour ago..."

Without moving, his expression shuttered, like he was locking things down for a sudden storm. It was his work face, and I realized that "craziest call" probably meant something different to a detective, and rarely something good.

"A surprising call," I amended. "An opportunity."

He relaxed, even looked rueful at his reaction. "Now you have me curious."

I told him everything about my conversation,

and he watched me closely as I shared. We polished off our drinks while he asked questions about the job, the hotel, and the type of work I'd be doing. The bartender brought us another round before I was done.

And the entire time, the energy between us hummed like a live wire. The same energy that had been there since we'd met, amped up by this shift in our status quo and my own residual high from the phone interview for the job in New York.

After so long without any changes in my life, now I had two giant ones competing for my attention.

John and New York, each tugging at me in different ways.

John's invitation to drinks tonight had upended my entire view of our relationship.

The New York phone call could upend my entire life.

John gave me butterflies and tingles around my heart and between my thighs.

New York made my pulse pound with possibility.

Tonight was thrilling and terrifying, that roller-coaster ride taking another loop.

"And then there's the fact that I like hotels." Hotels whisked you away from home and chores. They offered an escape. A private retreat.

"Big fan of hotels too," John said wryly when I took a deep breath to refuel.

Oh. I'd been rattling on while my mind spun and whirred, working on my dilemma. No wonder I'd stated the painfully obvious. *I like hotels?* How profound.

Except not.

John sipped his drink then nodded to mine. "You've hardly touched your second martini."

I let out a giddy laugh. It was probably 80 percent relief that I had a job prospect, but I felt light-headed and floaty, especially when John let his hand rest on the table, close to mine. "Are you trying to get me drunk, John Winston?"

"Definitely not." His eyes darkened as he said it, those two words loaded with implication. My breath caught at the taut intensity. In his stoic face, every flicker of response seemed magnified.

Because I knew that look was just for me. Just for this moment. It wouldn't be the same look tomorrow, or the next day.

That look said he definitely didn't want me drunk. It said he wanted me sober so he could do bad things to me.

I wanted that too, but I needed something else. Some clue as to what he thought about everything I'd unpacked here at the bar—the unexpected opportunity, and what I thought the move and the job might mean for me.

"Don't you have anything to say about New

York?" I asked. "About them headhunting me less than a day after I was fired?"

He took another sip of his drink as his gaze lingered on my mouth. "What's there to say? I'm not surprised. Your reputation is well earned."

Nice words, but they seemed so flat and left me feeling the same way. "You don't seem happy for me."

He paused, looking at his glass, seeming to choose his words even more carefully than normal. "I'm happy that someone appreciates you."

Had I missed something important while I'd been going on about New York? The attraction that had flared last night, the spike of desire when he'd leaned close, crowding me in between the car and his body—all of that was still between us, but tightly leashed.

"Yes, I like being appreciated," I said, still trying to gauge his reaction.

He raised his brows, slid his glass across the table, then swung around from his side to slide into the booth right next to me.

He'd picked up the gauntlet.

And I liked it.

"What are you doing over here?" My voice was breathy because I knew exactly what he was doing.

"Appreciating you," he said, skating his hand

along the back of the booth until his arm wrapped around my shoulders.

And, oh my. One simple touch. His arm. My shoulder. That was all, and he'd sent my temperature soaring.

My face was hot, and I knew I was flushed as I turned to face him, challenging him on purpose now. "Is that so?"

"Yes. But if you have doubts, let me make it incredibly, abundantly clear."

Anticipation wove through me as I waited for the thing I'd desired most from him.

I adored his friendship.

I cherished his camaraderie.

But I craved his touch.

So much that I was wound tight, tense and coiled.

So much that he filled my awareness, leaving no room for anything else. Inches away, his body blocked us from the view of most of the bar, but we could have stood in a spotlight and I wouldn't have attention left for anyone but him.

"How clear?" I asked, licking my lips.

He threaded his fingers through my hair, and I melted into him. At last, the man I wanted was touching me, and my body hummed everywhere.

"Perfectly clear," he rumbled, his voice as deep as the want in his eyes. "I'm going to do the thing I've wanted to do for the last year. So if you don't want me to kiss you, stop me now."

My breath caught, held, and came out in a soft, pleading command. "Kiss me now and don't stop."

My eyes floated closed, and his lips brushed mine, and the last year of longing faded away in the press of his mouth, in the taste of his lips.

In the tender but possessive way he kissed me.

His strong fingers curled around my head.

He took his time, exploring my lips, traveling across them, nipping and tasting.

And with each second that ticked by, I became more keenly aware of one thing—I wanted John more than I wanted New York.

Even if it wasn't going to last.

Even if he didn't feel the same wild beating in his heart that I did.

Because this kiss had been a year in the making.

This kiss felt like he wanted to memorize every detail of my lips, my skin, my taste. And I wanted that too.

Wanted him to know me in that way.

Because when John Winston showed how he appreciated me, oh hell, did he ever show me.

I—*we*—needed to get out of there soon.

Like, right now.

Because I was turned on beyond all reason, beyond any stopping it.

I broke the kiss, pressing my hands to his chest, thrilled that I could touch him this way at last. His chest was strong and firm under my touch.

And I needed to know how he felt wearing nothing.

"You know what I'd appreciate?" I asked, feeling bold. Feeling like no matter how uncertain my future was, my present was in sharp focus.

His lips curved in a grin. "I'm dying to know."

Curling a hand over his shoulder, I whispered, "Getting out of here. Right now."

9

MINDY

His place was closer.

In the elevator up to his condo, he roped an arm around my waist and yanked me close. "Do you have any idea how tempted I was to speed?"

"I bet it was tough," I said. "But you played the good cop."

His eyes shone with dirty deeds. "I did, but say the word, and I can play bad cop with you."

I liked that idea more than I'd expected to. "Are you saying you're going to cuff me?"

His hand cupped my ass, and he brought me flush against him. "I would very much like to." He dipped his head to my neck, licking a path along my skin that made me tremble. "But first, I'm happy to spread you out on my bed, strip you naked, and show you how much I appreciate every inch of you."

I moaned like a woman driven mad by desire.

I wanted it all with him. I wanted everything. Right then, though, I'd settle for John between my legs, fucking me hard.

The prospect of this calm, measured, in-charge man losing control was intoxicating.

When the elevator dinged, he untangled from me, and we stepped off, disheveled, hot, bothered, and eager as hell.

At his door, he grabbed his key but missed the lock.

"Locks are vexing," I teased, feeling sassy and powerful. Feeling like a woman about to get what she wanted.

He met my gaze. "*Vexing* is the deadbolt that's the last thing stopping you from getting the woman you're dying for under you and calling out your name."

A flash of heat flooded my body.

The key turned in the lock, and my pulse spiked. So did my ache for him as he pulled me inside, dropped his keys on the entryway table, and kicked the door shut.

Then he lifted me up, tossed me over his shoulder, and carried me to his bedroom.

John was just full of surprises.

But none of them were unwelcome.

He lowered me to the bed, tugged at the hem of my shirt, and pulled it over my head, groaning at the sight of my lingerie—a simple black lace bra. Then he lowered himself to me. "Do you have any idea how much I want you?" His voice turned rough and gravelly, and he was like a man unleashed.

The things he said.

The hunger in his eyes.

This was John unlocked, all heat and desire.

I laced my hands through his hair, so glad I finally could. "I bet it's as much as I want you," I whispered.

He crushed his lips to mine, kissing me in a whole new way, fevered, passionate.

And like he didn't want to stop.

Pulling back, I kicked off my shoes and scooted up on the bed.

He toed off his own and followed me, crawling over me, reaching for my wrists and pinning them over my head.

"I think you do want to play bad cop," I said.

"What I want is to have my way with you," he said.

My heart hammered with wanting, and desire coiled inside me, growing tighter, more intense. "Then have me," I said. "Any way you want."

He reached for my jeans, and soon we were unzipping, unbuttoning, tugging, and just tossing.

Pitching clothes onto the floor with abandon. Careless with need.

And I needed this man. I stripped out of everything, and his eyes blazed with a wild intensity as he drank in the sight of me.

"You are so fucking sexy," he rasped.

He shed his boxer briefs. My breath hitched as his cock sprang free, thick and hard.

He wrapped a fist around his length, stroking, and I nearly combusted.

"You are too," I murmured, entirely aroused.

And maybe he wanted to do bad things to me. Maybe he wanted to tie me up, to talk dirty to me, to have his way with me. But tonight, he seemed intent on one thing only.

Making me feel spectacular.

He reached for a condom from the nightstand drawer, rolled it on, and then gently but possessively spread my legs open. He rubbed the head of his cock against my wetness, and I groaned, letting my head fall back onto the pillow, savoring every single second of his touch.

Right then, I had no regrets about how long it had taken us to get to this place. Because all the buildup, all the longing, all the nights filled with the sinful temptation of John Winston had come to this.

To this man sinking inside me like it was the only thing on earth he wanted to do.

I gasped his name as he filled me. *"John."*

"Mindy," he whispered in return.

My name was sweet, but on his lips, it sounded filthy. And it had never suited me better.

The moment was perfect.

Made more perfect by the way he took control, stretching my arms over my head, gripping my wrists, kissing my neck fiercely as he fucked me.

Hard. Deep. And with so much passion.

He stared at me, his voice rough and hungry. "I have wanted you for so long. Thought about this so many damn times. Kicked myself for not taking you out sooner."

With each admission, he drove deeper, punctuating his truths with pleasure.

There was barely anything for me to say in return. I wasn't even sure I could form words. Not with the way he stroked inside me. Not with the way his hands gripped my wrists. Not with his words, smoky in my ear. "Spread your legs for me. Hike them up. Let me go deeper."

I did as he asked, and pleasure swept over me in wave after hot wave. He let go of my wrists, grabbed my thigh, and pushed my leg up higher still.

Opening me.

"Yes, that's so fucking sexy, so fucking perfect," he said.

Holy hell, did I ever feel appreciated.

Especially when he wrapped my legs tighter around his waist, pushed up on his hands, and gazed down at me. His lips parted, and he whispered my name like a prayer. Like a promise. "Mindy Gamble. I appreciate you more than you could ever know," he said.

His words unlocked me.

They sent my pleasure galloping to the horizon, to the far edge of want.

And then into bliss as I shattered, coming hard with the man who'd been an incredible friend.

Who was an even more incredible lover.

I expected him to follow me, but John was a determined man.

And he seemed determined to wring more pleasure from me first.

He flipped me to my hands and knees, banded an arm around my waist, and took me.

Just took me.

And if this was his bad cop, I wanted to be a very naughty girl.

He slid a hand up my back, grabbing my hair, tugging it.

I yelped, and he groaned. Then I surprised myself by saying, "Again."

He needed no more permission than that, grasping and tugging, pulling hard.

I moaned as pleasure built again, and my belly tightened.

He groaned too, sliding a hand between my

legs, stroking me where I wanted him most, and sending me tumbling toward another climax.

"It's so good," I breathed. "I'm close, so close."

"Come for me, sweetheart. I want to hear you a second time, the sounds you make."

It was the "sweetheart" that did me in.

The endearment in the middle of this excruciating ecstasy.

It was all I needed to fall off the cliff. He followed me there, his throaty noises thrilling me as he joined me on the other side.

He asked me to spend the night, and I didn't mention how it seemed inevitable that I would. I just appreciated his asking and said yes.

As he wrapped an arm around me, spooning me in the dark, he said softly, "You know what I think about New York?"

I tensed, worried what he would say. "What's that?"

"That you should spend as much time with me as you can before you go."

I was quiet for a moment, examining my conflicted reaction to that. Hell yes, I wanted to spend all my time with him while I had the chance. But at the end of it, would he really wave goodbye to me without looking back?

"They haven't officially offered me the job," I said, hedging my answer.

"They will." His arm tightened around me. "Any business would be damned lucky to have you."

It was the perfect thing to say, supportive and full of confidence in me. But it left me feeling empty all the same.

10

MINDY

I'd only flown to New York for a day, but it had been a long one, and I hadn't been able to nap on the plane. Bleary-eyed, I rode down the airport escalator, opening my Uber app as I headed for the exit. I almost missed John waiting by baggage claim.

Not true—there was no missing John anywhere, and no matter how tired I was, every nerve ending came alive as soon as I was near him.

Especially since this was unexpected and thoroughly welcome. He swept me into his arms and into a kiss that was all the more delicious because they were numbered.

"Well?" he asked when we broke it off for air and public decency. "How did it go?"

"Must have gone great," I said, "since they formally offered me the job."

"Not to say I told you so. But I did." Without a trace of smugness, he took the strap of my carry-on bag from me and put it over his shoulder. "Congratulations. This calls for a celebration."

"I have a few ideas how to do that." I waggled my eyebrows suggestively.

"So do I." He put his hand on the small of my back to usher me outside, where it was comfortably warm compared to the airport's air-conditioning. "Your place or mine?"

I laughed. "Mine, because I need a good night's sleep to tackle all the things I have to get done in two weeks."

John stopped walking, like he'd been rooted to the ground. "You have to move to New York in two weeks?"

A bit of alarm slipped through with his surprise, and I tried not to react to that as I answered. "I start in two weeks. It's sooner than I expected, but I can stay at the hotel until I find a place to live."

Was he upset by the thought of my moving away? If so, why couldn't he have said something in the bar on Saturday night, or in bed that night, or during any of the four days since? I'd asked his opinion about the job in New York, and he'd been so supportive and encouraging, but all he'd said about . . . *us* was that he wanted to spend all our time together until I left.

Or maybe the reality of my leaving had just

hit him. It hit me on the plane, somewhere above Kansas. Nerves and excitement had carried me through the day of interviews, meetings, and introductions. But once I slowed down, I realized I had to make this—*us*—work somehow. I had two weeks to figure it out.

"I'll be coming back and forth for a bit while I get settled. Planes fly both ways, you know." I bumped my shoulder with his to lighten the mood. "Miraculous flying machines they have these days."

He eased up on the frown, smiling almost sheepishly. "Good. It's hell going cold turkey on an addiction."

Addiction. I liked the sound of that. I liked being his sexy drug.

Wrapping an arm around my waist, John guided me out to his car. He couldn't have been waiting long, but he hadn't used any cop clout to leave his car in the loading-only lane. Always the model police officer in public.

In public.

I didn't hide a smirk. I had two weeks with John, and I wasn't going to waste any of them pretending I wasn't a cat with a cream smorgasbord.

As John navigated out of the airport, I steered back to a much earlier point in the conversation. "On second thought," I said, angling in the seat to face him, "since I have my overnight bag in the trunk, we can go to your place."

He glanced at me, that sexy hint of a smile curving his lips. "I thought you wanted to get a good night's sleep."

"Sleep is for the weak." And for people who had more than two weeks with someone I liked as much as I liked John. Though I was pretty sure I was feeling a whole lot more than *like*.

I would worry about my hatred of snow later. Not to mention the lack of John, whether for running or kickboxing or any other sweaty activities.

Only, as I watched him drive, streetlights and shadows painting his chiseled features, I faced one of many facts.

This move would be much easier if all I would miss about John was working up a sweat.

* * *

That night, after John turned "travel-weary" into "blissful exhaustion," he asked me my favorite things to do in Las Vegas.

"Besides you?" I'd asked, and he'd come very close to a smirk.

I'd brainstormed a list—restaurants, shops, and sights, both things I did often and things I didn't do enough—and we set out to check as many of them off as possible as part of the spend-every-moment-together plan.

Over the next several days, we ran our favorite route, bumping into K-9 Sergeant Jackson and his adopted dad. I'd find a new favorite route in New York, and new faces would become familiar, new regulars who'd get a nod or smile or some belly rubs. That was one of the things I'd wanted from this move.

John and I hit a few of my favorite eateries, but after each, I had to admit I wouldn't miss the diners as much as I would miss the company.

Tonight, we hit the blackjack tables at the Luxe.

I tapped my card to tell the dealer to hit me, but my attention was on John. I used to take my blackjack very seriously, when Brent and I would play. Tonight I sat catty-corner to John, trying to distract him by running the toe of my sling-back heels up the cuff of his trouser leg.

"You seem a little jumpy tonight, Detective Winston," I murmured, lifting a brow. "Expecting trouble?"

"Yeah," John growled, checking his new card. "I'm thinking there's some under-the-table deal-making going on."

"You're saying there's mischief afoot?"

He choked on a laugh, then shook his head, grinning at me. "The real troublemakers are the ones you don't expect."

"Some people are full of surprises." Propping my elbow on the table and my chin in my hand, I reached over and traced the back of his knuckles with a fingertip. This was as flirty as I got. I didn't pout or flutter my lashes. I didn't have a perfect manicure. But John had never seemed the type to go for those things.

"You're going to go bust," I predicted.

"You think so?" he asked, as casually as if I'd said it might be hot in Vegas today. "Are you fortune-telling now?"

My finger traced the tendons on the back of his hand. "Nope. I just know you're distracted."

He raised his brow. "Woman, I have laser focus. Or how else would I have resisted kissing you for the last year?"

"I'd wondered how you managed." Coolly, I drew a fingertip over his knuckles again, even though inside I was electric, knowing he'd had his eye on me the whole time too. "Me? I couldn't back down from a challenge, even from myself."

His eyes flashed with heat—a warning and a promise—but he didn't move his hand out of my reach. "You challenged yourself to resist this?"

"Well, sure, it seems pointless *now*," I said, drawing another smile from him. I loved being able to touch him—in private, in public, holding his hand above the table and playing footsie below.

As the dealer turned to us, I slid my toe under

his pants cuff, teasing until his free hand disappeared from on top of the table and landed on my knee, keeping me still.

He nodded for another card, and his fingers curved around my inner thigh. This would have been the night to wear a skirt.

John, looking unfazed, tapped his fingers on my thigh and lifted the corner of his new card for a peek.

He cursed under his breath, declaring himself bust.

I crowed with triumph, and John shook his head, flipping all his cards face down for the dealer to scoop up. Leaning onto my elbows, I came close to whisper, "You win some, you lose some."

He drained the last of his drink, his eyes never leaving my face as he set the glass down with precise care. "I haven't lost anything." His fingers on my leg inched a little higher. Nothing scandalous. Nothing anyone but the two of us would notice.

But, oh, did I notice.

"I'm on my way to a win, I'd say." His eyes strayed down to my cleavage, pushed up by the way I was leaning on my folded arms. "You win some, and then I win some, and then maybe you win some more."

"Big talk, big spender." I nodded to the impatient dealer. "He's waiting for you to ante up."

John gathered his modest stack of chips, tossed a tip to the dealer—extra for having made him wait—and stood, crowding me where I sat, and then crowding me closer with a hand on either side of the stool. "Now we're on our own time, and here's what's going to happen. I got a room here—because you like hotels"—his eyes glinted as he used my words to tease me—"and we're going to go up there, do not pass go, do not collect two hundred dollars, and *do* have hotel sex."

My blood rushed to the surface of my skin. Fiery. Tingly. Maddening. "And what exactly does hotel sex mean to you?"

"Sex where you can check your worries and inhibitions and bang like you'll have no regrets tomorrow."

I only pretended to think about it. Then . . . "Okay. I'm down for that."

"And trust me. I'm up for it." He wove his fingers through the hair at the base of my skull. "For you, always."

11

MINDY

The elevator couldn't go fast enough. "Why are elevators so slow in this town?"

"To seduce you to stay in the casino," he said, layering kisses across my neck.

"That makes no sense. We're already in the elevator," I teased.

"Does this make more sense?" he asked, threading his fingers through my hair and running a thumb across my top lip.

Heat flared wherever he touched, and sparks ignited in my chest. Technically, nothing about this fling, if you could call it that, made sense. How could he have this much effect on me already? How was everything so instantaneous and intense with him?

There was no rhyme or reason to it.

"I can't make sense of anything when you do

that," I confessed. "But it's a sexy kind of nonsense."

The doors slid open at the eighteenth floor, and we made it to the room without disgracing ourselves. As if making up for the slow elevator, the lock clicked on the first pass with the keycard.

We pushed inside, and the door had barely closed when John pinned me against it.

There was no other word for it. No other feeling like it.

For as long as I'd wanted him, I hadn't been fully prepared for the kind of lover he'd turned out to be.

It was no surprise that he turned me inside out with pleasure. I had feelings for him, and feelings do that to a woman.

But I hadn't expected him to be so . . . dominant.

And I'd never have guessed that I'd like it so much when he gripped my wrists, pushed my arms against the door, and pressed his deliciously hard body against mine. I was caged in and I didn't fight it, which was the complete opposite of Mindy during the day.

But Mindy at night liked being overpowered.

Loved it when he set to work stripping me.

Thrilled at the determination in his eyes and the rough murmur of praise.

So sexy.

So gorgeous.

Those weren't words I thought about myself. I wasn't decorative; I was the tough one. My body wasn't there to look at; it was a tool.

But John disarmed me. I didn't have to be tough. He seemed to like it when I was soft, when I gave in, when I let him have his way with me.

And his way amped up the electric charge between us.

Soon, he had me down to my bra and panties, and he let go of my wrists to make quick work of the buttons on his shirt.

I unzipped his jeans, freed him from his boxers, and stroked his length, feeling powerful in a whole new, sexy way when I touched him, when he gave in, groaning and thrusting into my hand until he muttered, "That's enough."

Then he rolled on a condom, hiked my thigh up to his hip, and wrapped my leg around his waist as he sank into me.

He let out a shuddery breath, and I gasped at that delicious moment when he was fully seated in me, holding there as I adjusted to him.

With one hand on my hip, he lifted my arms in the other, stretched them over my head, and fucked me like that against the door.

This was why hotel rooms in Vegas were dark and dimly lit.

For hotel sex.

For commanding men to take you against the door, to pound into you, to make you *feel*.

And with John, I was feeling so damn much.

Feeling as though he was marking me, claiming me in a way that was far more than physical.

"You," he murmured.

That was all.

But he poured everything into that one word, somehow making it convey everything that he wanted.

He wanted me.

I wanted him.

That was enough just for a while, to drown out the *tick-tick-tick* of the countdown to the end.

12
———

JOHN

Saturday afternoon, I was doing laundry to distract myself from the thought of Mindy back at her condo, boxing up what she wanted to store and marking what she wanted to move, when I got a text.

David: Going for a spin. You up for it?

I abandoned the laundry without regret.

John: Hell, yes. Usual place?

David: See you in thirty?

John: See you then.

Our usual place had a running path wide enough that I could jog alongside his wheelchair and not worry too much that a bicyclist would take me out.

Oh, they still tried—like that speed demon who came within inches of clipping me—but at least there was room to dodge.

"Watch it!" I warned, with a flashback to my days in a patrol car. The guy on the bike raised a peace sign without looking back.

Not breaking the rhythm of his gloved hands on the wheels, David said, "Kids these days, right?" He didn't bother to keep the laughter out of his voice.

I shot him a skeptical side-eye as I kept pace beside him. "Guy was fifty, at least."

He gave a quick laugh. "I'm talking attitude, not age."

David and I had been friends since our school days, since before the drive-by shooting that paralyzed his legs. His experience—violent crime coming to our neighborhood, David's life forever altered—was one of the reasons I'd gone into law enforcement.

"Ready for the last push?" I asked.

"Don't choke on my dust, Winston."

We saved our breath for the effort. David once observed that this stretch was where he had to have the right running partner. It had to be someone comfortable with not talking, and who kept the pace when society's conditioning said to slow down for the man in the wheelchair.

At the same point as always, we slowed to cooldown speed, finally stopping at a bench by the exit to the parking lot and stretching while our muscles were still warm.

"So, how long are Lucy and the kids out of town?" I asked. His wife and daughters had gone with his in-laws to the West Coast.

"They'll be back tomorrow night." He stretched his right arm across his body, then his left. "It's weird having a Saturday with no soccer games or chores to be done at home."

"I refuse to believe Lucy didn't leave you a list."

"Okay, then, a Saturday without my beloved wife making sure I got my part of the chores done."

David's wife was a good one. She reminded me a little of Mindy—practical, straightforward, took no shit. And for a moment, a pang tugged under my ribs. A kick from some part of me that said, *Pay attention. You want some of what he's having.*

A list of chores? If it came from Mindy, yes.

Someone I missed when she went out of town.

Someone who returned to me.

But Mindy was going away, and I couldn't imagine sharing a list of chores with anyone else.

"Anyway, I'm already tired of pizza delivery," David said. "You want to grab dinner tonight?"

I had plans with Mindy—a plan to grab all the time I could while she was here. David and I hadn't hung out in far too long, but he'd still be there after she'd left.

"Hot date, huh?" Then he leaned forward in his chair to peer at my face and said, "Aha! You do."

"Well, I have a date to play mini-golf. I don't know about hot, since the only things swinging will be putters."

"Mini-golf," he echoed, liked I'd shattered his illusions about my sexy bachelor life.

I shrugged. "Mindy loves it. It's kind of her thing, so I'm taking her to play then to grab drinks afterward at one of her favorite bars."

"Wait up." He held up a hand. "This is Mindy? Mindy from kickboxing? Mindy-who-pops-up-in-conversation-suspiciously-often Mindy?

"I only know one. But we were just friends until recently."

"You'd mentioned that." Tapping his temple, he gave a sage nod. "But I logged the information as a curiosity."

"If you're so curious, you should join us. Mindy's heard about you too."

He shook his head. "Call me crazy, but I'd rather not interfere with your swing. Mini golf, or anything else." I rolled my eyes as he cleared his throat before venturing on. "But I would like to meet her, since sooner or later you're going to need my relationship advice."

I blinked, startled by the word. And I was rarely startled. "It's not a relationship."

But saying that was painful. I hadn't thought beyond making a move while I had the chance. I knew she'd made her decision to move, so I hadn't let myself even think the word "relationship."

"She's leaving town in just over a week."

"Hmm. So, sooner instead of later, then."

He was joking, but not really. I was going to have to deal with these feelings—and I did have feelings for her, all kinds of feelings. I wasn't sure about taking his *advice*, but it would be nice if I wasn't alone while I grappled with this.

"Don't give up hope, John. You don't give up on a work challenge or a physical challenge. You don't have to give up on an emotional one."

Why did he have to use the words "give up," dammit?

Because he knew me that well, of course.

I scrubbed my face with my hands, scratchy with

dried sweat. "All else aside, I'd really love for you to meet her. I'll text you the details of the bar." I'd offered the invitation impulsively, but it was deliberate this time. If there was a hope in hell of making something work here, I was going to need advice.

He must have sensed it, because he agreed.

* * *

"And then John peppered the cop with question after question." David had joined us for a round of drinks after Mindy and I enjoyed a round of mini-golf. With her encouragement, he was recounting the greatest hits from our childhood —in this case, when a police officer had visited our fifth-grade classroom for Career Day.

"The rest of us just wanted to get outside for recess, and he wouldn't let up. But not even the risk of being pummeled behind the jungle gym would deter him."

Mindy laughed. "And did he stare lovingly at the guy's badge too?"

"Like he'd discovered buried treasure," David said, then took a drink of his beer. "All of the gear —you'd think he got to handle Batman's utility belt. Especially the handcuffs. Eventually, he got a pair and practiced picking the lock while they were off, while they were on . . . I never doubted he'd eventually become a cop."

"That's 'Detective' to you, sir," I added, deadpan. "Show a little respect."

David rolled his eyes. "When you earn it, I will."

I leaned back in my chair where I could see them both, Mindy and my best friend, teaming up against me. I was damned glad they'd met, and I hadn't realized how much I needed to see that look on her face tonight—happy and in the moment, grinning like it made her cheeks hurt.

I needed to store up this snapshot for later, when she was gone and there weren't any more. We hadn't discussed whether she'd come back to visit, and that had been purposeful. Sure, we'd mentioned the possibility of a visit here or there, but we hadn't had *the talk*. Maybe because I wasn't sure what to say, or what I could truly offer her. Whether I could offer her what she deserved.

Eventually, we said good night to David, Mindy bending to give him a hug as if they were longtime friends. Over her shoulder, where only I could see it, David mouthed, *Sooner or later.*

He was right. Ignoring my feelings didn't make me immune to them. My life and my job would be a lot easier if I could pick and choose what to feel. But I couldn't.

Mindy and I walked slowly to my car. I didn't like to leave until David had gotten situated behind the controls of his van—I was always impressed by how he folded his wheelchair and lifted it in after himself—but I tried not to loiter too obviously. Once he'd left and we were in my car, she arched a playful brow. "So, can I see your badge, Detective?"

Her fingers traced an outline over the place on my shirt where a badge would go if I were in uniform. I caught her hand and held it against my chest. "Ms. Gamble, are you trying to get under my utility belt?"

"What if I am, Officer?"

I let her go and turned the key in the ignition. "Then I'd say it's not my badge you need to see. How about the cuffs instead?"

"Deal." Her light-speed answer made me laugh, and made the drive to my place seem way too long.

Because the way we were together—the way I wanted her, no matter what happened when she left – wasn't meant for sooner or later.

It was meant for *now*.

13

MINDY

He slammed the door shut, and there it was—the dark look in his eye. The side of this man no one else got to see.

The cool, calm detective—unruffled, laconic, self-possessed—was a different man after dark.

Intense, commanding, and . . . voracious.

I was the object of his desire, and that thrilled me.

He turned me around and pressed my cheek to the door, lingering at my back and whispering into my neck, "You have the right to be fucked hard."

"I'd like to exercise that right, please, Detective," I said in a throaty purr that left no doubt I was down for this as long as he didn't stop touching me.

He undressed me completely, then yanked my

wrists together, slapped on the cuffs, and marched me to his bedroom.

Hottest perp walk ever.

We reached the bed, and he gave me a little push so I landed softly on my stomach. With one knee on the bed beside me, he undid the cuff on one wrist, took both my hands, and lifted them above my head. The click was so loud as he fastened the cuffs around the headboard and closed it around my other wrist again.

"Lift your ass for me," he said.

And I did, offering myself on all fours.

I was bound to his bed, unable to move my arms, naked and with my ass in the air. I must have been out of my mind.

But when he moved behind me and licked a path up one leg, lingering decadently on my thigh, the sound he made suggested he was the one barely holding on to his wits.

He was the one who needed control, I suspected, as he cupped each cheek with one hand, spread me open, and then dipped his face between my legs, licking my wetness. He pulled me along with him to madness, because I was out of my mind with desire too.

The sounds I made were criminal.

The noises he made were obscene.

There were no words, just grunts and growls from him, and moans and sighs from me.

This man I was falling for devoured me, and

my mind went hazy. My world narrowed to only this—the sheer bliss of him consuming me with that wicked tongue until I was shouting, crying, and coming so damn hard.

He didn't uncuff me.

He left me bound to the headboard, and I craned my neck to watch him strip. To watch him take off his shirt, undo his jeans, sheath himself with a condom, and then cover me with his strong body, finally sliding inside.

"Ohh," I moaned. "That's..."

"Incredible," he whispered in my ear as he moved, slow but purposeful, leaving me with an exquisite ache on each thrust.

It didn't feel like fucking.

This felt like connecting.

Like true and honest intimacy.

Like John was letting me see another side of him.

How he needed it. How he wanted it. And as he stroked faster, his breath coming harder, I knew it was more than simply a craving for dominance in the bedroom.

"It's never been like this," he rasped out as he neared the edge.

It wasn't just a release for him.

It was us, the way we came together.

14

MINDY

The only concessions I wanted for the night before I left for New York were that I got to choose the restaurant—my favorite dim sum place—and where we would spend the night—his place, where there weren't boxes to remind us I was getting on a plane tomorrow afternoon.

There was no argument from John, except for a spirited discussion about how I ate more than my share of pot stickers and how that wouldn't have been a problem if we'd gotten two orders like I'd suggested. It escalated to a chopsticks duel as we both tried to grab the last one from the basket. Laughing didn't make it easier.

I was going to miss this so much.

Would miss John desperately.

Would miss the *us* that we were now and the *us* that we could become.

But those were tomorrow thoughts.

Tonight, I wanted to zoom in on the moment. The connection. The chemistry.

Because John's hands were busy. On my knee. Then my thigh. My arm. Now, as we were finishing, he ran his hand through my hair.

This.

My God, I would miss it. And there was no point hiding that. "I'll miss this," I said.

"Me too. All of this." He took a beat, as he seemed to be thinking. "Will you come back at all? To visit, maybe more than here or there?"

My heart beat faster. We were circling the thing I wanted most—a chance with him. Any chance with him was better than no attempt at all.

"I would, if you wanted me to."

He leaned in and brushed his lips against my cheek. "I would. I definitely would want that."

He wasn't asking me to stay, but a long-distance relationship made more sense anyway.

It was more logical.

More doable.

It was incredibly possible, and I felt a little lighter, a little better knowing he might want it too.

Part of me was terrified to ask for more, knowing that more could lead to heartbreak. But it might also lead to something wonderful.

I swallowed down my fear.

"So do you want to try a long-distance relationship?" I asked, putting it out there, because that was the only way to know.

His smile spread nice and easy, just the way I liked it. "Funny that you asked, because I was going to suggest the same thing."

Okay, I was a little bit giddy now.

Even more so when he threaded his fingers through my hair and drew me close for a kiss.

When the kiss ended, I took a breath, straightening my shoulders.

"I'll stake out some interesting eateries for us to try when you visit," I said, trying to make this as normal as possible. To think of this as the beginning of long-distance John and Mindy and not the end of Las Vegas John and Mindy. "And we can go to our old favorites when I come here."

John grabbed a dumpling. "It's cute how you think we're going to leave the bedroom when you visit."

"We're going to need nourishment at some point."

"There is nothing you can't get delivered in Vegas. It's gotta be the same in New York. Maybe even more so."

I'd run through all the scenarios already—it would be harder for him to get away, so I might have to do more of the traveling. And as much as I loved the sexy times—and, oh hell, did I love them—we weren't hormone-driven teenagers.

Phone calls and FaceTime could hold us between visits.

"On the subject of places for things to be delivered..."

John raised his brows as I overstretched the segue, but he waited for me to go on.

"I've decided to hold on to my condo and sublease it for now." I kept my tone casual, but it was a pretty big signal—if he wanted to see it. I tried not to search for any clues to his reaction. I wanted cautious optimism, to match my own feelings, but as long as it wasn't outright rejection, I could work with it.

After a thoughtful beat, he said, "So you've decided not to decide yet?"

Oh, he had me pegged. I laughed at myself, and at how he'd deciphered my reasoning a lot quicker than I had deciphered it myself.

"New York is just a step on the ladder. I'm not sure yet where the next step will be. Maybe I'll get this hotel property set up and running smoothly, and then move on to another one in a few years."

And who was to say that might not be in Vegas?

That was what I wanted to get across without putting pressure on him by saying it straight-out.

For a man with such a stoic demeanor, there were all kinds of things going on in his expression. Things I couldn't fully read but desperately wanted to. So desperately that I was afraid I'd see what I wanted whether it was there or not.

"Mindy . . ." He reached for me again, sliding his hand to the back of my neck.

His phone rang before he could finish. Which was a shame, since it looked like it would be something good.

He let go of my hand and pulled out his cell. His grimace when he saw the screen was a shame too, for a different reason. There wasn't enough panic for it to be Sophie in labor. That meant work was on the line.

He'd once said the quiet since closing the Thomas Paige case was like waiting for the other shoe to drop.

I was pretty sure I heard a *thunk*.

"Go ahead," I said with a smile to reassure him. "I'm not going to make a dash for it while you're on the call."

"Hopefully it's something small." Then into the phone, he said, "Winston here."

I caught a few words—*ten million, found unconscious, APB,* and *outgoing flights*. That wasn't trivial.

It was sounding less trivial every minute. Finally, he hung up, and I wasn't surprised when he said, "I have to go."

"Of course you do, John." I'd already signaled the server for the check and moved my napkin from my lap to the table. "The waiter is bringing the check, but if you need to leave right away, I can wait on it and call for an Uber to get home."

He was quickly locking into work mode—I imagined his mind was already at the crime scene—but he registered the offer and came back to the moment with a crooked smile that made everything in me clench. "It's not so urgent that I'd be off the hook if I skipped out on the bill."

Then that hint of humor vanished. He paid the server in cash, and we headed out, his hand on my lower back like he didn't realize he was keeping contact with me as long as possible.

When we were outside, he finished a quick text then turned to me. "I can drive you home, at least."

I shook my head. "I'll feel better if you just go ahead."

He grimaced. "You didn't want to stay at your condo tonight." He took out his keys, starting to pull one off. "Here. Go to my place. I might still make it back before morning."

I frowned, but not for myself. "That bad, huh?"

Running a hand through his hair, he said, "Yeah. No one killed, thank God, but a hell of a lot of money gone and a couple of casino owners out for blood. FBI is already sniffing around. It's going to open a whole can of worms, and I'm really sorry—"

"John." I caught his hand because I needed him

to hear this. "I was military, remember? I know all about drop everything and go." I pressed his hand between mine, then stretched up to kiss him gently. "I understand. Though I think I'll stay at my place tonight. Now, go do your thing."

He trailed his hands down my body and took a step back.

"I'll see you tomorrow."

"You'd better."

Then he was gone—first mentally, like he'd flipped a switch to focus on the task ahead, and then the rest of him, heading to his car at a jog.

I watched him as I reached into my purse for my phone to call for a ride. I'd glimpsed his quickly hidden surprise when I didn't freak out about him bailing on me. But truthfully, I couldn't imagine getting bent about him doing his job, doing what he had to do. If he wasn't somebody who would pay his tab and jet when he was needed, he wouldn't be the man I'd fallen for.

That was right. Fallen.

I thought about it all the way home, up to my condo, and then some more as I changed and half-heartedly looked for things to put in either my suitcase or a storage box. I wished I were a last-minute packer. Then at least I'd have the distraction of a packing frenzy while my heart crumbled along with my plans.

Because as I peered around, the staggering truth of my emotions hit me.

I loved John. It was a hell of a thing to admit right as I realized my plan for having it all was not feasible. Long-distance John and Mindy were not a viable option for the same reason that I loved him—his devotion, his loyalty, his drive.

It would be hard enough to coordinate our schedules for weekend visits. Trying to coordinate time together with a variable like crime in Las Vegas? That would be nothing but frustration and misery.

In Las Vegas, I'd have all of John who didn't belong to his job and his sense of duty and justice. But moving to New York, I wouldn't have that much. I would only have a tiny piece of him.

I never pictured myself as someone who would change her plans for a man. But neither had I pictured myself as someone who wouldn't adapt. Life was about finding the work-around when shit happened. Happiness was about being your best self, and for the very lucky, that meant bending over backward to keep your partner—that person who *made* you your best self—around as much and for as long as you could.

I closed my eyes for another long minute as I sat on my couch in my stripped-down living room, surrounded by boxes marked to move or store, give away or throw away. When you had to pay to transport or store something, you found out what was actually important to you.

What you could walk away from, and what was worth any cost.

John was worth the cost. I wouldn't walk away from him if he were mine.

All it would take was a word.

Stay.

Just ask me to stay.

15

JOHN

Last night was the kind of night I loved and hated.

Loved because I absolutely loved my job.

Hated because some greedy fuckers had lifted more than ten million dollars.

But hated even more because of how I'd had to leave Mindy.

And now I needed to figure out what to do with the storm of emotions in my chest.

My sister set a mug in front of me, and I eyed the steaming liquid. Just when I'd thought life couldn't look any more bleak. Tea. Fucking tea.

"Don't you have any coffee?"

She patted her belly. "Pregnant, duh."

"Did I mention I got an hour of sleep on the couch at the station?"

"You did." She sipped from her mug. "Doesn't make me any less pregnant."

"Doesn't Ryan drink coffee?"

"He loves me too much to make me smell it when I can't have it." Her look said I should take a lesson from that.

I sighed and sipped the tea. How could a hot beverage taste so girly? Sophie spread polka dots and ruffles like other people spread a cold.

"So, talk to me," she said, cupping her mug between her hands. "And explain to me why you're such an idiot."

"I've been explaining for the last quarter-hour."

"You've been telling me that you don't want Mindy to leave but you don't want to ask her to stay."

Was it wrong to glare daggers at a pregnant woman when that woman was your sister?

"It isn't right to ask her to stay. Not when I can't give her everything. All of me." I sighed and slumped in my chair. "I'm married to my job. Clichéd, but true."

"What did Mindy say when you had to leave last night?"

I was silent as I tried to remember. I'd taken the call from work. I'd told her I had to go. And she'd said . . .

Of course you do, John.

A statement of fact. Not biting or sarcastic.

I understand. Now, go do your thing.

And then I'd kissed her and left.

Sophie, on a roll and not waiting for an answer, set her mug down hard enough to rattle the table. "You did tell her why you weren't begging her to stay in Las Vegas, right, John? Explained how conflicted you felt about asking someone to share whatever you could spare from your first obligation?"

"That's just it." I pointed at her. "This thing with Mindy was able to grow because I was in the downtime. The lull between cases. But this new case is going to be involved and protracted. And after this, there will be another one. I can't tell how long there'll be in between, but I do know the case will always come first."

"John." Sophie leaned onto her elbows and looked me in the eye. "Do you think you're the only one who has an important job? It's not like Mindy wouldn't know what she was in for. She was engaged to a soldier, right? You think she didn't know she might lose him to something a lot more permanent than an important case? Maybe you need to get over yourself."

I gaped at her, realized my mouth was hanging open, and closed it with a click. "That's why I can't ask her to take that on again. Cop marriages fall apart all the damned time. Plus, there's the inherent risk in the job. And then there's what's best for her. This job in New York is a life-changing opportunity. A write-your-own-ticket kind of deal. That's important to her, and it's not fair to ask her to stay."

Sophie slid her hand across her kitchen table and covered my hand with hers. Even though her life revolved around Ryan, she'd always made a point of drawing me into it too, so we wouldn't lose moments like this.

"You are my brother, and I love you, John. But that's just baloney. Of course it's fair *to ask* her to stay. She can say no." She patted my hand, and I recognized condescension when I saw it. "I know it seems strange, but a woman can say no to a man."

The door clicked, and Sophie called over her shoulder as Ryan walked inside, Ajax bounding by his side. Ryan was sweating, and the dog had his tongue lolling out, looking like they'd just finished a morning run. "Isn't that right, sweetheart?"

As the shepherd trundled over to give Sophie a hello lick, Ryan went straight for the sink, pouring a glass of water and downing it quickly. "Of course that's right, my beautiful peach."

I took my turn petting the pooch and eyed Ryan as he set down the glass in the sink. "Do you even know what she's talking about?"

"Nope." He walked over and kissed Sophie's cheek. "I just know she's right."

My sister smirked at me. "If he wasn't so smart, I wouldn't have married him."

Ryan ran a palm over her hair. "Seriously though, John? The big secret to a relationship? Never assume. The joke is always that a man can't read a woman's mind. But they can't read ours either."

"See?" said Sophie, smiling at her husband. "Such a genius."

Ryan leaned into Sophie for another kiss. "Sorry I can't stay and help you sort out your happy ending, John. I need to shower, then I have a meeting with a client, and he's paying for this genius."

"Go get 'em, tiger." Sophie rubbed her belly in a soothing circle. "Baby needs a new pair of shoes."

I flicked my gaze back and forth between them. That kind of love seemed so reachable and so unattainable at the same damn time.

Sophie turned back from watching Ryan head down the hall and caught my unguarded expression as the dog slumped to the floor, panting. Her own expression softened, and she took my hand again.

"All you can do is tell her you love her," Sophie said, squeezing my fingers. "Don't assume you know what she wants or that she knows what you want. Talk to each other, be clear about your feelings, and you'll figure out the rest."

"As we go? Just figure it out as we go?" I let my

horror at that show in my face, and she flicked the back of my hand with her fingernail. "Ouch!"

"Suck it up, brother mine." She leaned her elbow on the table and her chin in her hand, resting the other one on her watermelon belly. "Look at Michael and Annalise. She's in Paris, for heaven's sake—a country *and* an ocean away."

"Not the same thing. They live here half the year and there the other half. They're only apart for a few weeks when they travel for work."

"But they figured that out after they said *I love you*." She laid her hand on my arm and squeezed. "Everything stops and starts with *I love you*, John. Set that as your cornerstone and you can build just about anything around it."

With those words branded on my brain, I left.

But the whole way to my car, I replayed her final piece of wisdom.

It seemed too simple.

Hell, it was simple.

It didn't solve everything, but maybe it solved what mattered most—don't assume.

Let the woman know.

Be honest.

And then figure out the rest.

Could I do this?

As I got in my car, I asked myself one more time if I could.

And the answer was remarkably easy.

Mindy was worth it. Oh hell, was she worth it.

16

MINDY

Everything would be all right.

I had a plan. I'd text John tonight to let him know I'd settled safely in my hotel room. He'd asked me to do that when he messaged this morning at zero dark thirty to say he didn't know if he'd make it over before I had to leave.

John: Just in case I can't get there. But I'll still try.

Mindy: Hey, I know you'll be fielding calls and emails from the FBI and all that. I'll be back in two weeks. We'll see each other then.

And then he'd ghosted me.

I'd grown tired of checking my phone for a

response, sending myself a text to check that the system hadn't crashed, watching the news for any story about a heist. I only cared that my two former places of employment were unaffected, and that I might get a glimpse of John.

Was that what I was going to do in New York? Follow #casino_heist on Twitter for news, maybe look for a picture of him in a CNN splash photo?

It was time to get myself together. I closed and locked my suitcase, looked around the tidily stacked boxes, and made sure the lights were off and everything was unplugged.

I was inventing things to do to delay leaving.

I closed the door, double-checked the lock, grabbed my suitcase, and headed downstairs.

When I reached the lobby, John was coming through the doors from the Strip.

I froze.

He didn't.

He marched over to me and took my suitcase from my hand, not asking, just ordering. "You can't go anywhere today."

"I beg your pardon?"

Honestly, I tried to be offended, outraged, indignant. But inside, not even that deep down, I was gleeful and giddy.

Because he was here.

Because he'd stopped me from leaving.

Because he sounded like after-dark John when he growled like that. I wanted nothing more than to hear that growl and know it was for me. *All mine.*

He carried my suitcase to the elevator.

"What's going on?" I asked.

The suitcase hit the floor with a thump as he dropped it and turned to me, putting his hands on my shoulders and running them down to my fingers, then up again to cup the back of my neck.

"Please stay. I want you to stay. Stay with me because I'm lost without you. Because I love you and I hope to God you're in love with me too."

My heart flew, beating too fast, winging away. That was all I'd wanted—for him to ask me to stay.

I pressed my lips to his, whispering against his mouth, "I'm so in love with you too."

He drew me closer for a quick, hot kiss. Then he stroked my cheek possessively. "So, you're staying. Here. With me. And I'm going to give you everything I can while I can. If that's not enough, then ... we'll figure it out."

"Figure it out ... on the fly?" I gave an exaggerated gasp. "You, Detective John Winston? I'll have to see it to believe it."

"Believe it," he promised in a gravelly rumble. His hand slipped around my waist and held me close. "I didn't have a clue what I was going to do when I got here. I just drove and hoped I'd figure it out before I did something stupid like let you leave without knowing that I wanted you to stay.

I didn't want to let you get away. I don't ever want you to get away from me."

Wrapping my arms around him, I confessed, "I was almost stupid enough to leave."

"But you're here." A soft, butterfly-weight kiss.

"I'm here." And being here required more kissing. Lots more kissing.

I tugged him close, sweeping my lips over his, stepping onto this brand-new path with a kiss and a promise, and he made me one in return.

"If you really want the job in New York, we'll make long-distance work until we figure out something better. But I don't want you to go." He kissed me again and again, as if trying to convince me when I'd already decided. "I want you to stay. You're so good to me. You get me. You understand me." He rubbed my arms as if he could tell I was cold everywhere he wasn't touching. "I can be that for you, Mindy. I want to be enough of a reason for you to stay in Vegas, and if you do, I can help you figure out where you want to go from here. Will you let me?"

"You'll be enough," I whispered. "You *are* enough. You and I together will always be enough."

I didn't know what I'd be doing about the job other than obviously giving it up.

But this was worth it. *We* were worth it. He was my partner, and we'd put our heads together and figure it out.

But first, there would be staying-together sex.

And when he took me up to the bedroom, stripped me to nothing, and pinned me, I counted *that*—his passion—as another damn good reason for staying.

EPILOGUE

Mindy

A few weeks later

Ajax bounded across the dog park to greet me with the kind of tail-wagging, playful-bowing, tongue-swiping joy that only a dog can manage.

Right behind the beagle was Ryan, also headed my way. I started to crack a joke about the life lesson of appreciating a drool-slimed tennis ball, but a look at his face changed my mind. He hadn't called me here to joke around. His brows knitted with stress or worry, and something serious flitted through his eyes.

"Is everything okay?" I asked. "Is Sophie okay? Is she in labor?"

He nodded, then shook his head. "Yes, everything is okay; no, she's not in labor. As of five minutes ago, at least."

I scratched Ajax behind the ears as the dog sat beside me. "So, it's really any minute now, huh?"

Another nod, more decisive this time, a tired grin showing through the clouds of whatever had brought him here. "My first kid is coming. *Our* first kid. God willing, the first of many."

"I know I'm job hunting, but my nannying days are behind me," I said playfully.

Something seemed to strike him as ironic there. "Actually, that's what I wanted to talk to you about."

"Nannying?"

"Not exactly." Ajax pawed the ball he'd dropped politely, reminding us about it. "It is about work though. With Michael being out of town half the year, and with business booming, it's become harder for me to devote all the time I need to our local clients."

I stood up straighter, just like Ajax did when he spotted his ball. If I had ears like his, they'd prick forward. I had a sense where this was headed, and it was hard to hold back a grin.

"Plus, you're about to have a little bundle of distraction in the house," I pointed out. "Another bundle of distraction," I added as Ryan picked up the tennis ball and threw it for the dog.

"You nailed it exactly." Ryan stroked his chin thoughtfully. "I'm kicking myself for not realizing this sooner, but, Mindy, you'd be a terrific partner in the business. And there *is* that rumor on the street that you might be available."

I tried to contain my glee. This was the perfect gig—working with people I respected, doing the job I loved, in the city I called home.

As a partner.

There was no playing it cool.

"I accept," I said, extending a hand to shake on the deal before anything could change his mind.

Though it wouldn't, because yeah, I *would* be an excellent partner.

Ryan laughed. "You don't want to hear the terms?"

"Of course I do, but I'm going to accept."

Shaking his head, he picked up the ball Ajax had brought back. "That's a terrible negotiating tactic."

As we strolled through the park, he outlined what he was thinking in terms of the partnership, and he already looked less stressed. Even if I hadn't shown my hand immediately, this was such an obvious fit that my yes was just a formality.

I had a very good feeling about today. Today,

and a lot of days going forward. It was a gorgeous afternoon, the park was full of snouts and tails and optimism, and it seemed like all the reasons why I was meant to be here, to stay here, lay in front of me. I knew it wouldn't stay that way, but at that moment, my path was as clear as the sidewalk leading to the gate of the off-leash area.

Sophie waited just on the other side of the fence. Ryan was texting—telling Michael what we'd agreed—and didn't seem to immediately notice the way she leaned a white-knuckled hand against a fencepost for support.

"Ryan," I said, nudging him to encourage him to look up. "I think your moment is here."

Sophie's eyes connected with her husband's, and the whole story played out in a look. *Here we go. Our next adventure. You and me, in it together.*

Timing really was everything.

"Go on, partner." I gave him another elbow bump. "I'll take care of your dog."

"Thanks." He didn't meet my eyes as he rushed out the gates—he only had eyes for his wife.

He hurried over to Sophie. Taking her hand and elbow, he guided her toward the parking lot, telling her the hospital bag was in the car.

Oh boy. I hoped they weren't in the Aston Martin.

Ajax trotted to the gate then looked back to me, figuring things out. I picked up the slimy tennis ball, and he loped over. The holder of the ball had authority, it seemed.

We went to find John standing with some volunteers from K-9 Buddies and, more importantly, some of their dogs.

This had been John's idea, formed after our running into retired K-9 Sergeant Jackson and his person. A two-birds-one-stone idea. The meet-and-greet would raise awareness about the service-dog adoption program as the volunteers conducted some education on safety—how to approach a strange dog and the importance of training. Things that a responsible dog person should know, whether they owned a dog or not.

Plus, the dogs got to interact with people and socialize with non-working dogs, and there was nothing like watching an all-business dog learn how to play.

Tossing the ball for Ajax, I sidled up to John, who introduced a retired lieutenant colonel to me. She squatted down by a gray-muzzled doggo, scratching his belly with a gleam in her eye, like a teenager spotting a boy band.

Pretty sure John had a hidden talent as a dog matchmaker.

He tugged me over to the big-dog area and pointed out the dogs romping there. I spotted a shepherd mix with markings like spectacles. He was calmly and intently watching as Sergeant

Jackson and Ajax tussled, the three-legged dog holding his own just fine.

"Who's that?" I pointed to the serious dog on the edge of the group.

"That is Holmes."

He didn't offer any elaboration. "As in, Sherlock?"

"I'm not sure. He was with a K-9 police officer. Retired early because he got cataracts."

So, the spectacles were ironic? The universe was a strange place.

"Can surgery fix that?" I asked.

"The shelter is hoping to raise money to cover it."

Just then, a gleeful Ajax jumped onto Holmes, and I held my breath, worried that there would be a fight to break up. But Ajax made a play-bow to Holmes with his slimy ball between his feet. Holmes looked unconvinced about the offer. He moved closer. The dogs circled, sniffing tails, and—

Fake out! Holmes grabbed the ball and ran off with it, and Ajax gave chase.

I laughed. "Oh my God. Did you see that? That dog has some game."

John's mouth curved into a huge grin, and he couldn't take his eyes off Holmes. "Yeah, he does. I guess we'll be seeing a lot of it."

Because he had game too.

And obviously, Holmes was coming home with us.

* * *

It had been a day for adding to families.

The next afternoon, we visited John's niece in the hospital.

I tried not to play favorites with my nieces, but Isabelle Sloan was the most adorable baby I'd ever seen.

Especially in John's arms.

That might contribute just a bit to my bias, because I couldn't stop thinking how good he looked like that, holding a tiny creature who needed him.

Oh hell, heart. You need to settle down.

We adopted a dog yesterday. We still hadn't arranged our combined furniture in the condo. Every choice we'd made, it was clear, so clear, that it was the right one.

But babies were a different story.

* * *

Or maybe not.

Because a few weeks later, after four days of queasiness and an offhand joke from John, I picked up a test at the drugstore. And once I convinced John that *I* was not joking, I did what I needed to do.

He waited with me, watching the stick like it was a suspect about to break a case wide open. Finally, it turned.

The evidence?

Two pink lines.

I gasped, and John? Well, his face lit up with the biggest smile I'd ever seen.

I hadn't planned on this.

We hadn't planned on this.

But I hadn't planned on getting fired or chucking a perfectly adequate job offer in order to stay with the man I'd fallen in love with either.

His expression, his radiant happiness, told me the unexpected was worth it. The baby was unplanned and completely wanted, late nights and long hours be damned.

"We're having a baby," he said in wonder. Then he slid me a sheepish look and admitted, "I was hoping it'd be positive."

"You were?"

Just like *I love you*, it surprised me until he said it, and then it seemed so obvious.

He smiled. "I was. I never thought I'd say that, but the second you felt sick to your stomach, I was hoping this was why."

So his joke hadn't been a joke so much as a wish.

Same here.

Because as soon as I saw those lines, I knew I wanted this as much as if we'd planned it.

He drew me in for a kiss, consuming my lips with a whole new wave of possessiveness.

When he let go, he nodded toward the door and the world outside our bubble.

"What do you say to marrying me tonight?"

I knew exactly how to answer. "I say yes."

ANOTHER EPILOGUE

Mindy

Five years later

I pulled into the parking lot of the Thomas Paige Memorial Library with my husband, who immediately hopped out and opened the car's back door to undo the seat belt for Amelia and then for her younger brother, Jackson.

It was storytime, and Amelia never wanted to miss a word.

I didn't either, because it was a chance for all the kids to see each other. One of many, but we never took any opportunity for granted.

I hoisted my son onto my hip. "This little guy is getting bigger by the second."

John took Amelia's hand and looked both ways before we all crossed the parking lot. "Good. We can make him start walking the dogs soon."

"I like walking the dogs," Amelia said.

"Me too," Jackson chimed in. If his big sister liked something, it was a sure bet he'd like it as well.

We went inside the library and found our friends and family in the children's section, where Brent and Shannon sat in beanbags while their three kids scampered through the shelves. Where Colin wandered among the books with his seven-year-old daughter, a girl he and Elle had adopted from foster care. Where Sophie, in a peach dress, cooed at baby Olivia, their third daughter, and my business partner Ryan had parked himself in a kid-size chair that somehow held his weight as he read a book to his two older girls.

Michael and Annalise wandered in after John and me. They didn't have kids of their own, but that was by choice. They were perfectly content with each other, they'd said, and they had no shortage of nieces and nephews who they loved spending time with.

My throat hitched with happiness.

The groundbreaking five years ago for this

library had set so much of my new, wonderful life into motion. That day stood for all I had hoped my friends and now my family would enjoy.

Peace, love, and happiness.

The Sloans had come far.

And so had I. From that moment, I'd come into a new chance, a new love, and a new family all my own.

This man had once been my sinful temptation, and now he was my friend, my lover, and my husband.

He was mine, always.

And even though sometimes he worked long hours, and sometimes he was stressed, and sometimes—well, oftentimes—I worried about him, it was worth it.

Loving was always worth it.

Eager for more sexy romance? Try my new emotional, forbidden and sexy standalone The RSVP. It's FREE IN KU!

I've written more than 100 books! **All of these titles below are FREE in Kindle Unlimited!**

The Love and Hockey Series

The Boyfriend Goal

A roommates-to-lovers, teammate's little sister hockey romance!

The Romance Line

An enemies-to-lovers, player and the publicist, forbidden romance!

The Proposal Play

A brother's best friend/marriage of convenience romance!

The Girlfriend Zone

A coach's daughter romance!

The Overtime Kiss!

A single dad/nanny romance!

The Flirting Game!

A neighbors to lovers, fake dating romance!

Hockey Ever After

Just Breaking the Rules!

A brother's best friend/workplace/one who got away romance!

Just Playing for Keeps!

A grumpy sunshine, fake dating romance!

Holiday Romances

Merry Little Kissmas

Fake dating my brother's best friend at Christmas!

My Favorite Holidate

Fake dating the billionaire boss at Christmas!

Darling Springs

It Seemed Like a Good Idea!

An only one-bed-in-the-room, forbidden, small town bodyguard romance!

I've Got a Crush On You!

A grumpy sunshine, workplace romance where the boss has a secret identity!

The My Hockey Romance Series

Hockey, spice, shenanigans and cute dogs in this series of standalones! Because when you get screwed over, make it a double or even a triple!

Karma is two hockey boyfriends and sometimes three!

Double Pucked

A sexy, outrageous MFM hockey romantic comedy!

Puck Yes

A fake marriage, spicy MFM hockey rom com!

Thoroughly Pucked!

A brother's best friends +runaway bride, spicy MFM hockey rom com!

Well and Truly Pucked

A friends-to-lovers forced proximity why-choose hockey rom com!

The Virgin Society Series

Meet the Virgin Society – great friends who'd do anything for each other. Indulge in these forbidden, emotionally-charged, and wildly sexy age-gap romances!

The RSVP

The Tryst

The Tease

The Dating Games Series

A fun, sexy romantic comedy series about friends in the city and their dating mishaps!

The Virgin Next Door

Two A Day

The Good Guy Challenge

How To Date Series (New and ongoing)

Friends who are like family. Chances to learn how to date again. Standalone romantic comedies full of love, sex and meet-cute shenanigans.

My So-Called Love Life

Plays Well With Others

The Almost Romantic

The Accidental Dating Experiment

A romantic comedy adventure standalone

A Real Good Bad Thing

Boyfriend Material

Four fabulous heroines. Four outrageous proposals. Four chances at love in this sexy rom-com series!

Asking For a Friend

Sex and Other Shiny Objects

One Night Stand-In

Overnight Service

Big Rock Series

My #1 New York Times Bestselling sexy as sin, irreverent, male-POV romantic comedy!

Big Rock

Mister O

Well Hung

Full Package

Joy Ride

Hard Wood

Happy Endings Series

Romance starts with a bang in this series of standalones following a group of friends seeking and avoiding love!

Come Again

Shut Up and Kiss Me

Kismet

My Single-Versary

Ballers And Babes

Sexy sports romance standalones guaranteed to make you hot!

Most Valuable Playboy

Most Likely to Score

A Wild Card Kiss

Rules of Love Series

Athlete, virgins and weddings!

The Virgin Rule Book

The Virgin Game Plan

The Virgin Replay

The Virgin Scorecard

The Extravagant Series

Bodyguards, billionaires and hoteliers in this sexy, high-stakes series of standalones!

One Night Only

One Exquisite Touch

My One-Week Husband

The Guys Who Got Away Series

Friends in New York City and California fall in love in this fun and hot rom-com series!

Birthday Suit

Dear Sexy Ex-Boyfriend

The What If Guy

Thanks for Last Night

The Dream Guy Next Door

Always Satisfied Series

A group of friends in New York City find love and laughter in this series of sexy standalones!

Satisfaction Guaranteed

Never Have I Ever

Instant Gratification

PS It's Always Been You

The Gift Series

An after dark series of standalones! Explore your fantasies!

The Engagement Gift

The Virgin Gift

The Decadent Gift

The Heartbreakers Series

Three brothers. Three rockers. Three standalone sexy romantic comedies.

Once Upon a Real Good Time

Once Upon a Sure Thing

Once Upon a Wild Fling

Sinful Men

A high-stakes, high-octane, sexy-as-sin romantic suspense series!

My Sinful Nights

My Sinful Desire

My Sinful Longing

My Sinful Love

My Sinful Temptation

From Paris With Love

Swoony, sweeping romances set in Paris!

Wanderlust

Part-Time Lover

One Love Series

A group of friends in New York falls in love one by one in this sexy rom-com series!

The Sexy One

The Hot One

The Knocked Up Plan

Come As You Are

Lucky In Love Series

A small town romance full of heat and blue collar heroes and sexy heroines!

Best Laid Plans

The Feel Good Factor

Nobody Does It Better

Unzipped

No Regrets

An angsty, sexy, emotional, new adult trilogy about one young couple fighting to break free of their pasts!

The Start of Us

The Thrill of It

Every Second With You

The Caught Up in Love Series

A group of friends finds love!

The Pretending Plot

The Dating Proposal

The Second Chance Plan

The Private Rehearsal

Seductive Nights Series

A high heat series full of danger and spice!

Night After Night

After This Night

One More Night

A Wildly Seductive Night

Joy Delivered Duet

A high-heat, wickedly sexy series of standalones that will set your sheets on fire!

Nights With Him

Forbidden Nights

Unbreak My Heart

A standalone second chance emotional roller coaster of a romance

The Muse

A magical realism romance set in Paris

Good Love Series of sexy rom-coms co-written with Lili Valente!

I also write MM romance under the name L. Blakely!

Hopelessly Bromantic Duet (MM)

Roomies to lovers to enemies to fake boyfriends

Hopelessly Bromantic

Here Comes My Man

Men of Summer Series (MM)

Two baseball players on the same team fall in love in a forbidden romance spanning five epic years

Scoring With Him

Winning With Him

All In With Him

MM Standalone Novels

A Guy Walks Into My Bar

The Bromance Zone

One Time Only

The Best Men (Co-written with Sarina Bowen)

Winner Takes All Series (MM)

A series of emotionally-charged and irresistibly sexy standalone MM sports romances!

The Boyfriend Comeback

Turn Me On

A Very Filthy Game

Limited Edition Husband

Manhandled

If you want a personalized recommendation, email me at laurenblakelybooks@gmail.com!

BE A LOVELY

Want to be the first to know of sales, new releases, special deals and giveaways? Sign up for my newsletter today!

Want to be part of a fun, feel-good place to talk about books and romance, and get sneak peeks of covers and advance copies of my books? Be a Lovely!

CONTACT

I love hearing from readers! You can find me on Twitter at LaurenBlakely3, Instagram at LaurenBlakelyBooks, Facebook at LaurenBlakelyBooks, or online at LaurenBlakely.com. You can also email me at laurenblakelybooks@gmail.com

www.ingramcontent.com/pod-product-compliance
Lightning Source LLC
LaVergne TN
LVHW012109070526
838202LV00056B/5672